INTO THE FLAMES

THE YOUNG UNDERGROUND

INTO THE FLAMES

Robert Elmer

BETHANY HOUSE PUBLISHERS
MINNEAPOLIS, MINNESOTA 55438

Cover illustration by Chris Ellison

Published by Bethany House Publishers
A Ministry of Bethany Fellowship, Inc.
11300 Hampshire Avenue South
Minneapolis, Minnesota 55438

Printed in the United States of America.

Library of Congress Cataloging-in-Publication Data

Elmer, Robert.
   Into the flames / Robert Elmer.
      p. cm. — (The young underground ; #3)
   Summary: Their work delivering newspapers for the Danish underground lands twins Peter and Elise in a Nazi prison where they experience firsthand the importance of faith.

    1. World War, 1939–1945—Underground movements—Denmark—Juvenile fiction. [1. World War, 1939–1945—Underground movements—Denmark—Fiction. 2. Denmark—History—German occupation, 1940–1945—Fiction. 3. Brothers and sisters—Fiction. 4. Christian life—Fiction.] I. Title. II. Series: Elmer, Robert. Young underground ; #3.
PZ7.E4794In   1994
[Fic]—dc20   94–24906
ISBN 1–55661–376–8   CIP
                                               AC

To Rhonda—
My wife and writing partner.

CONTENTS

DANGEROUS DELIVERY

"Come on, Peter. Don't look so serious. We're just out delivering bundles of laundry, remember?"

Peter's twin sister, Elise, looked back at him and tossed her long blond hair as she started to skip. Peter hurried his steps to keep up with her, pulled up the collar of his coat against the cold, and shivered.

Just bundles of laundry. Almost true, but not quite. He could feel the heavy stack of illegal newspapers hidden inside the bunch of shirts he had under his arm. These were the kind of newspapers the German army had outlawed ever since the war started in Denmark. The kind that told the truth about what was happening in their little country. The kind that could get them into big trouble if anyone found out.

"Hey, wait up, Elise!" Peter tried to walk faster on the slick sidewalk, but he skidded around like a tipsy figure skater.

Peter's sister had already turned the corner on the busy street, skipping through the sea of bicyclists and dark-coated walkers on their way home from work. He knew the way to Sundberg's Dry Cleaners as well as she did, but Peter slowed down to circle around an old woman who planted her cane right in front of him.

"Excuse me!" cried Peter, tripping over her cane. He lost his balance on the icy sidewalk, and the precious package flew from his arms. Before he knew what was happening, his shirts were all over the sidewalk in front of the startled woman, and the small, single-sheet newspapers were drifting through the crowd like leaflets dropped from an airplane. Peter was mortified, but not because of the shirts.

"Young man!" The woman looked up and started to scold Peter, then she caught sight of one of the illegally printed Underground newspapers. Her eyes lit up. *"The Free Dane?"* She looked at him sideways. "You're a little young to be this kind of paper boy, aren't you?"

Peter shrugged. He was twelve, after all, which didn't seem too young to him. But what could he say? The woman picked up a copy of *The Free Dane* for herself and helped Peter gather up a few more. Others in the crowd stopped to help while Peter got down on his knees in the slush and frantically scooped up the shirts and the rest of the papers.

"Sure, take one," he told each person who stopped. One man—Peter thought he looked about his dad's age—took two handfuls and stuffed them into his coat pockets.

"For the office," mumbled the man. Peter thought he had just about all the papers gathered back up or given away when he heard a snicker behind him. It was a laugh he had heard before, and Peter closed his eyes for a moment. *Keld Poulsen,* he thought, and the back of his neck bristled.

"You missed one, Andersen." Peter turned around to see Keld holding out one of the papers in his beefy hand. The boy's fingers matched the rest of his body: puffy and always dirty. Even though they were in the same grade at school, Keld was a year older, meaning he had been held back at least once. And Peter didn't know how Keld managed to eat so much, especially now during the war when everyone was supposed to be rationing food. Keld always seemed to be chewing on something.

Still on his knees, Peter didn't want to look up at the older boy. As soon as he reached out to take the paper, Keld dropped it over a puddle of slush. Peter grabbed for it, but someone else was too quick. Out of the corner of his eye, he noticed someone come up behind him, reach down, and snatch the paper. It was Elise, and Peter breathed a small sigh of relief.

"Come on, Peter, let's go," said his sister.

Peter didn't need any convincing. He rose to his feet and brushed off his soggy knees. Keld just stood there with a smirk on his face, chewing on his cheek.

"Come on, Peter," mimicked the older boy. "Better go now and play newspaper boy with your sister." Then he laughed, a kind of chuckle that normally made Peter close his eyes and shake his head. "Just don't get caught."

Peter and Elise said nothing, only turned and walked down the street as quickly as they could. "Thanks, Elise," Peter mumbled to his sister. "That Keld . . ."

"It's okay," she replied. "We can't let him think we're scared of him."

Keld had always given Peter the creeps, but this was even worse. He got the feeling that Keld was more than just the class bully. There was something else to his voice, something darker. He imagined the boy following them, or spying on them from around a corner.

They were in the oldest part of the city now, where the cobblestone streets were narrower. Around the corner was the ancient Saint Mary's Catholic Church, which was over five hundred years old. At least that's what Peter's Uncle Morten told them before he was captured by the Germans. Uncle Morten had taught them all about the old buildings in the city.

But today there was no time to be a tourist. Peter and Elise slowed down before they reached Sundberg's Cleaners, where they would drop off their papers. They stopped for a moment in front of the music store next door, pretending to look at the sheet music displayed in the window.

In the front window of the cleaners, which Peter could see out of the corner of his eye, a vase of flowers meant all was clear. But a bare window meant that someone was in the shop—possibly a German soldier—and they should wait to come in. Peter glanced casually to the side, trying not to look too obvious.

"The flowers are a little wilted today," observed Elise as she led the way into the cleaners. Peter followed his sister inside, and they hoisted their packages up to the counter.

"Mr. Sundberg!" Elise's clear voice blended with the gentle tinkle of bells from the door. But the owner was already shuffling up from the back door, past hangers of suits and skirts and shirts. He mopped a wisp of hair back from his forehead and smiled when he saw them.

"Some more shirts for me?" he asked, the same way he did every time they came. But as he glanced at Peter's package, he paused for a moment and wrinkled his brow. "What happened here?"

Peter was afraid the man would ask. "Well, I had a little accident. I got most of the papers picked up, except people that were helping me took a few. I thought it would be okay." Peter wasn't sure how Mr. Sundberg would react.

The man's expression changed at once as a customer walked in the door. He was all business. "I understand," he told Peter and Elise. "Only please be careful not to drop these shirts again." He caught Peter's eye and paused a second to make his point. Peter understood.

Then Mr. Sundberg shoved two more bundles of shirts over the counter toward them (only without any newspapers packed inside) and turned his attention to the woman who had walked in. Peter tucked his brown paper parcel under his arm and was about to leave with his sister when Mr. Sundberg put his hand on the package.

"Wait a minute, kids." His voice sounded different, more urgent, and he was looking past Peter's shoulder out into the street when he said it. Without giving Peter and Elise a chance to look, he pulled them around the counter and bent down to whisper in their faces. "Out the back door with you now!" he ordered them, motioning toward the rear of the store with his head. "Hurry!"

The only thing Peter could think of as he and Elise hurried through the cleaning shop past racks and racks of clothes was that Mr. Sundberg had seen someone coming. Elise pushed open the door to the alley and paused for a moment to look back.

"What do you think's going on?" she asked. The sound at the front door of the shop answered her question. As the twins stood frozen in the doorway they heard what they didn't want to hear: The door slammed open, and several men yelled something in German. Mr. Sundberg's voice sounded as if he were apologizing for something, trying to explain. Then came crashes and the sound of breaking glass. More yells.

Peter and Elise looked at each other. "Nazis!" they whispered at the same time. Peter quickly but carefully shut the door behind them, and they raced down the alley with their packages. They turned onto King Street, then Mountain Street, and didn't slow down until they reached their own neighborhood on Axeltorv Street.

Breathing hard, Peter looked for the things that told him he was close to home. Clausen's Bakery where his mother sent him to get bread every morning. The little shoe repair shop that always smelled like leather and shoe polish. Next came their apartment, and Elise gripped his arm.

"Nothing about this to Mom and Dad?" she whispered.

Peter wasn't sure if it was a question or what. He sighed. They were doing the right thing—at least he thought they were. Sometimes he just wanted to tell his parents everything. But what would they say?

"Remember, Peter, this is the only thing we can do for Uncle Morten," Elise said quietly as she followed him up the stairs to their second-floor apartment.

"I don't get how that's supposed to work," he answered. "Us

delivering papers three times a week isn't going to get him out of jail."

"But everybody's just doing little things. Don't you get it, Peter? We're doing a little thing too, and it all adds up." Peter thought Elise sounded more like his teacher, Mrs. Bernsted, than his twin sister. That's why he and his friend Henrik—his Jewish friend who had escaped the Germans more than a year before— called Elise "The Brain."

Peter counted the steps as he neared the top. Twenty-three, twenty-four, twenty-five. "Yeah, but I think I'd rather do something bigger, like . . ."

"Like what?"

"I don't know." He stopped on the stairs for a moment, trying to figure out what he had meant. "Just something bigger, like really getting Uncle Morten out of prison. Aren't the Resistance people doing *those* kinds of things?"

"Peter, that's silly." When Elise talked at him this way, Peter felt as if his mother were scolding him for not making his bed or something. "What are we supposed to do," Elise went on, "just walk right up to the German guards and say, 'We want our uncle out now'?"

"You forgot to say please," added Peter. It wasn't funny that their uncle was in prison and had been for more than a year. And it wasn't funny that he had been captured for helping Peter's friend Henrik and a boatload of other Jewish people escape to Sweden. It was just that Peter couldn't think of anything else to say that would make it better.

Elise smiled for a second and pushed Peter up the last two steps. "When you think of a good idea," she told him, "let me know."

Peter simply nodded and closed his eyes as he put his hand on the doorknob of their apartment. For a second, he could picture Mr. Sundberg in the cleaning shop—cautious Mr. Sundberg—being taken away to the same place they had taken Uncle Morten. No, it wasn't funny at all. Then he could see Keld standing over him when he was picking up papers, and something clicked.

"Elise?" He turned to face his sister. "How do you think the Germans found out about Mr. Sundberg?"

Elise shook her head and wrinkled her eyebrows. "I don't know, Peter. There's a lot of people out there. Someone might have seen something."

"Like me dropping the papers all over the place?"

"Well, yeah, but then they would have followed us. I don't think that had anything to do with it."

"What about Keld Poulsen? Don't you think maybe he has something to do with it? He's creepy."

"I don't know, Peter. We just have to be careful. Come on, Mom and Dad are probably wondering where we are. Here, let me put those in my backpack." She reached over and took his bundle of shirts from him and stuffed them with her own bunch into her schoolbag.

Peter turned back to the door, but the thought wouldn't escape him. For as long as he could remember, Keld Poulsen had always taken a personal interest in trying to make him miserable. Peter had never figured out why. But this was bigger, much more serious. There had to be another reason for what happened that afternoon.

Pretty soon, Elise, he thought. *Pretty soon we're going to have to tell Mom and Dad.*

SEARCHING FOR CLUES

From her spot in front of the stove, Mrs. Andersen swept her hand at Peter and Elise to quiet them down as they tumbled in from the stairway.

"Your dad's on the phone," she whispered, her finger to her lips. Then she signaled with one finger toward the closet.

"Mr. Andersen's coat belongs in the closet, don't forget." Whenever Peter had to do something, his mom called him "Mr. Andersen." So Peter launched his coat over at Elise, hoping she would catch it. His sister sidestepped the flying brown coat, let it fall on the floor, and smiled sweetly at him.

"Mr. Andersen can hang up his own coat," she echoed her mother.

"Thanks." Peter puffed out his cheeks and made a fish face at Elise, but he walked over to the coat and picked it up. On the other side of the room, Mr. Andersen made "Keep the noise down" motions with his hand, just like his wife had when Peter and Elise walked in. Peter found a wooden hanger for his coat and looked over at his dad.

"You're not going home from work today? Okay, that's fine,"

Mr. Andersen told the phone, plugging his free ear and closing his eyes. He spun on his heel and rocked as he strained to hear what the other person was saying. "I'll just let myself into the apartment. I still have a key."

There was a pause as the other person said something. "Uh-huh, right. We'll be sure not to touch a thing except for the filing cabinet in his . . . oh, you've stored it all in which closet? Sure, I know which one. I just have to . . ."

Another pause. Mr. Andersen nodded and fidgeted with the wire to the phone receiver. "Right, I just have to find that insurance paper. His insurance company called me at work the other day, and I had to explain to them that he was on a long vacation overseas. They knew exactly what I meant." Then he grunted, said a few more words, and hung up the phone. He walked over to Peter and ruffled his son's hair. Peter didn't try to duck.

"Hey, it sounds like a circus when you two walk in the door," teased Mr. Andersen, half seriously. "When I'm on the phone—"

"Sorry, Dad," offered Elise. "I'll see that my brother keeps it down next time."

"Your brother?" Peter replied. "You make just as much noise." He threw a pillow from the couch at her, which hit her square on the back of the head.

"Okay, okay, could everyone stop this argument long enough to wash for dinner?" asked Mrs. Andersen, raising her voice. She was stirring something in her speckled blue kettle on the small two-burner stove, something that smelled to Peter like the soup they had eaten the day before. *Lentils*, he thought, but he didn't dare complain. Actually, his mother's soups tasted pretty good most of the time, even if she didn't have a lot of groceries to work with.

"Who was on the phone, Dad?" asked Peter after they had all sat down.

"Oh . . ." Peter's father looked up from his bowl. "Just the fellow from the bank who's staying in Morten's apartment while—" He looked away, put down his spoon, and rubbed his forehead.

"I have to go over there for a minute to take care of some papers."

"Hey, Dad . . ." Peter pushed the hot soup around his bowl, watching the steam drift up. "How about if Elise and I come along? Maybe you need some help or something?" He waited for his father to turn him down.

Mr. Andersen just cleared his throat while Elise gave Peter a "What are you doing?" expression. She looked as if she didn't have the slightest notion what Peter was asking, or why. He didn't either, really; he only had a fuzzy idea that if they saw the apartment, they could somehow find out something—anything—that might help Uncle Morten.

"Well, I—" Mr. Andersen shrugged. "I suppose it's okay, as long as you don't have anything to do for school. I have to go right after dinner."

"Great," replied Peter, blowing on a spoonful of hot soup before sipping it.

———

Elise followed Peter into his room after they had finished eating and leaned up against the doorway.

"What are you thinking, Peter Andersen? Are we playing detective now?"

"Not playing, Elise." Peter laced up his shoes and tried to tie together two halves of a shoelace that had snapped. "I just thought that we haven't been to Uncle Morten's apartment since he was captured, so maybe we should go there to make sure there isn't—"

"Isn't what? What do you expect?"

"I don't know! Something. Anything." Peter felt himself getting irritated with his sister. "I really don't know what we'd be looking for. I don't even know if I would know when we found it. I just thought it would be a good idea to go check things out, that's all."

Elise blew her breath out and combed her fingers through her long hair. She had let it grow past her shoulders over the last few months. Sometimes when Peter was annoyed with his sister, he wondered what would happen if she went through a doorway and the door slammed right behind her. But he'd never dare say it out loud; she was taller and stronger than he was.

"Okay, fine," she finally agreed. "Only I don't want to snoop in Uncle Morten's personal things."

"We're just going to go see," promised Peter as he bundled up for the quick walk over to their uncle's apartment. Five minutes later he and Elise were following their father down the sidewalk.

"I hardly remember what Uncle Morten's apartment looks like, it's been so long," Elise said as they tried to keep up with their father's quick strides.

"Sure you do," Peter told his sister. "Remember the view of the harbor and all the paintings of sailing ships on the walls? And lots of neat books?"

"Oh yeah, I remember now." Elise stuffed her hands into her coat pockets to keep them warm. "You know, I think he needs a wife to fix the place up—make it more homey."

"A wife?" asked Peter. The thought had never occurred to him.

"Yes," replied Elise. "I think we should help him find a wife."

Peter opened the flap of a red street mailbox and let it clang shut as he walked by. "Well, first we have to get him out of prison, don't you think?"

"You're starting to sound like our crazy cousin Kurt." She crossed her arms as they slowed a few paces behind their father and dropped her voice to a whisper. "We can't get Uncle Morten out of prison—we've already talked about that once. I don't even know what I'm doing, going along with you to his apartment like this."

"Just looking for clues, remember?" Peter thought back to the summer when he and Elise had spent their vacation with their aunt and uncle and cousins. His younger cousin Kurt was always the first to jump headlong into an adventure. Back then, Peter had been the cautious one, the one who was always scared. Now he was still just as afraid of German soldiers, but something was prodding him to take risks—like help with the Underground newspaper. Peter thought his sister was the same way, only she didn't want to admit it maybe.

They reached the entrance to Uncle Morten's apartment building, went through the front door, and took the stairs two at a time up to the second-floor landing.

"Now I don't want you kids touching anything," their father called at them as they clattered up the stairway. "We're storing most of Uncle Morten's things in one room, but the furniture is still his."

"Doesn't the guy who's living there now have his own stuff?" Peter asked. He thought it was kind of odd that someone had just moved in, as if he were Uncle Morten.

"He's a friend of your uncle's," replied Mr. Andersen. "From the Un—" He paused. "Well, he's a friend, that's all. Kind of apartment-sitting."

Peter caught his father's slip of the tongue and looked over at Elise to see if she had heard too. "From the Underground," Peter was sure his dad was going to say. Elise looked as if she hadn't heard.

"His is the first door on the right." She pointed to number 201 on the front of a door. "I remember now."

"Right," answered their father, who was fiddling with a key to open the door. A minute later, he straightened up and turned the key around in his hand.

"That's funny," he told them. "This door was left unlocked."

He pushed open the door and flipped on the light, but didn't go in. Instead he just stood in the doorway, stared, and groaned. Peter and Elise tried to look around their father to see what he was staring at, but he held out his hands to block their view.

"What's going on, Dad?" asked Elise.

"I don't know," said their father in a blank sort of voice that scared Peter. His father put down his arms, letting them hang limply at his sides. "I don't know."

But it didn't take long for Peter and Elise to see what their father was staring at. Inside the apartment, furniture was pulled over, clothes were ripped from drawers and strewn across the floor, and everything that had once been on a shelf was scattered wildly. Paintings were slashed, and books were ripped to shreds. Peter's father leaned over limply in the doorway.

"I can't believe it," he repeated. "I just can't believe it."

Peter and Elise gripped their father's shoulders, afraid to go in.

"Burglars, Dad?" Elise finally asked. "We should call the police." Her father straightened up and held them both by the hand. Then he took a careful step inside.

"Not burglars," he said, pointing to a large swastika someone had painted on the mirror with something that looked like lipstick. "Nazis. They always leave their ugly calling card."

Seeing the German symbol made Peter grind his teeth. He thought it was like seeing a cross, but twisted and disfigured into something that didn't look anything like a real cross at all. And it was all over their country—on flags, on the armbands of German soldiers, everywhere. He wanted to tear them all down. Instead, Peter had to turn away for a moment in disgust.

The three of them picked their way through the ruined apartment, ankle-deep in scattered papers and books. There were tears in Elise's eyes.

"Why would anyone do something like this?" she asked her father. "Uncle Morten never hurt anyone."

Mr. Andersen just shook his head and picked up a few of his brother's files.

"Obviously"—he picked up a paper—"they were interested in something here. I'm not sure what, but it probably has something to do with the kind of people your uncle was involved with before he was taken to prison. Maybe names, addresses of Underground contacts." Then he shrugged. "Who knows?" He looked up for a moment, as if he had just remembered something.

"I had no idea it would be like this," he continued. "You two shouldn't be here at all."

"It's okay, Dad," said Peter. "Maybe we can help you clean up."

They spent the next hour sorting through papers, picking up books, trying to straighten up shelves.

"Look at all these books," said Peter, picking at a pile of up-turned volumes next to a spilled bookshelf. "Why would anyone bother to make such a mess, unless they were looking for something special?"

Mr. Andersen waded into a pile of file folders on the floor in front of a closet. He picked up a few and started looking through papers in the living room, while Peter and Elise concentrated on straightening a stack of books in their uncle's bedroom. Elise got down on her knees and looked behind a larger shelf that hadn't been torn down.

"Hey, Peter," said Elise, reaching behind the shelf. "His Bible."

Peter looked at the book Elise held in her hand.

"Looks as if it's the only book in the whole apartment that hasn't been ripped apart," observed Peter. Elise leafed through the worn black book.

"It's sure used, though," she whispered, examining the pages. "He's got it all marked up—notes in the margin, underlines, everything."

"I guess he reads it a lot," said Peter. "Or he used to. Here, let me see."

Peter took the worn volume and leafed through the pages himself. Elise was right about the book being well used. Peter's own Bible at home was still as new looking as the day he got it from his grandfather, two years back. Peter started to read one of the tiny handwritten notes in a margin when a scrap of paper slipped out and drifted to the floor. Elise bent to pick it up.

"Hey, look at that," said Peter, taking it from his sister. "A clue."

"Clue to what?" asked Elise. "It's just a bookmark or something. Put it back."

"No, wait a minute," insisted Peter, straightening out the little note. "It's someone's name and address. Maybe this was what they were looking for." He read it quietly, Elise looking over his shoulder to see. He pulled the book the other way.

"I thought you didn't want to know," he told her.

"Oh, come on," replied Elise. "What does it say?"

"All right." He held up the small paper for her to see. " 'Lisbeth von Schreider, South Beach Street 45-B, Thursdays at 7:00.' "

"That's it?" asked Elise, sounding disappointed. "That doesn't tell us anything."

"Sure it does. It's a contact. Maybe somebody from the Underground that can help us, someone who knows for sure where he is. We can't be certain that he's still at Vestre Prison." He stuffed the scrap of paper into his pocket and handed the Bible to Elise just as he heard his father close the filing cabinet in the other room.

"Are you two done snooping around?" Mr. Andersen called in to them. Then he poked his head into the bedroom where they were standing. "I'm ready to go home now."

"We just noticed his Bible," volunteered Elise, holding the book up for him to see. "Do you think it would be okay if I borrowed it for a while, just until Uncle Morten comes home?"

Mr. Andersen shrugged his shoulders. "That's fine," he replied. "Your uncle isn't using it too much right now. You can return it to him when he . . . uh . . . gets back. We've done all we can—at least for now. I left a note for the fellow who's staying here so he won't be shocked. Let's get home."

They followed their father back out of the apartment and dragged themselves home the way they had come. Peter could still picture his father's horrified look when he saw the trashed apartment, but now Mr. Andersen had returned to his usual cool expression. It was odd, thought Peter, how his father could pretend as if nothing had happened just minutes after a big shock.

Before they went up the stairs to their apartment, their father turned around and put his hands on Peter's and Elise's shoulders.

"I'll explain to your mother what happened. Do you understand?" With a serious expression he looked from one to the other. "She's worried enough as it is."

"You'll tell her, though, right?" Peter wanted to make sure. With all the secrets going around lately, he would have liked telling a few to his parents. It was getting harder and harder to keep everything in.

They couldn't tell anyone about delivering Underground newspapers. They couldn't even know the real names of the people they worked with. And they surely wouldn't tell anyone else about the ransacked apartment. Sometimes Peter felt like a bottle of soda someone had shaken—and now he was ready to explode.

"Yes, I'll tell her." Their father's voice brought Peter back to the present as they climbed the stairs.

There was one more thing, if Peter could slip it in before they got to the door.

"Dad?" he squeaked. "Do you know anyone named Lisbeth?" The words came out meekly as they approached their front door.

"Lisbeth? No, I don't think so. Who's that? Someone from school? A girlfriend?" He winked down at his son.

"No . . . I don't know. I just saw the name and wondered."

"Saw the name where?"

"In Uncle's Morten's apartment—in his Bible. I thought it was somebody you might know."

Peter's father turned serious for a moment at the mention of Uncle Morten. Then he nodded, as if remembering something. "Oh, *that* Lisbeth. Yes, he was dating a girl named Lisbeth before he was captured. Quite seriously, I think. Your mother and I met her once, and he talked about her a lot. Seemed real nice, even though I think she comes from a German family. But I haven't heard a word about her since."

"You don't know where she lives?" asked Peter.

"No, I wouldn't know that. But that doesn't mean anything.

Your uncle has a lot of friends I don't know anything about."

    Maybe we'll have to find out, thought Peter as he followed Elise into their apartment. He slipped his hand into his pants pocket once more to make sure the note was still there. Not that it mattered. He had it memorized.

MYSTERY MEETING

"Elise, it's been two days since we had to run out of the cleaners," Peter complained to his sister. He had his nose in a book, but he couldn't remember where he had left off. "When do you think we're going to deliver again?"

"I told you we have to be patient," Elise explained once more. "And don't bounce on my bed." She reached over from where she was sitting at her little desk and tried to close the book in his face. "Bent, the guy from the newspaper, told me that we just have to wait, and that they're looking for a new drop-off place. I worry about poor Mr. Sundberg, though."

Peter stopped bouncing long enough to find his place in his book. "Me too. I hope they're going to let him go." He read another page, then looked up at his sister again.

"Maybe we could just take a couple of piles of the papers and pass them out," he told her. "I did that when the package dropped, remember? Lots of people would take them."

"Yeah, and look what happened with Keld," she reminded him. "Did you forget about that?"

Peter didn't say anything for a moment, just put his finger on the page and closed the book. "No, I didn't forget. And I didn't forget about that Lisbeth von Schreider lady, either. We should find out exactly who she is."

"That's just like your idea to go get Uncle Morten out of prison, Peter. What do we say to her? 'Hi, we're Morten's niece and nephew, and we thought you could tell us the magic password to get him out of jail'?"

"Come on, Elise. I didn't say that. I just thought the name was a clue, that's all."

"Well, if it is, tell me what you think we're going to do with it."

"How do I know?" Peter shrugged. "I haven't figured that out yet. I thought maybe The Brain would come up with something."

Elise smiled. He hadn't called her that for a long time, maybe since Henrik had escaped to Sweden.

"Well"—she walked to the window, pressed her nose to the cold glass, and breathed a patch of fog—"maybe we can think of something."

Peter opened his book again and held it open with one hand while he let his right hand dangle beneath Elise's bed. His hand brushed what felt like a small pile of books, and he pulled one out.

"Hey, what's this?" he asked. "Looks like a diary or something."

Elise grabbed for the book, but Peter was too quick.

"Give it here!" she insisted. "That's mine."

"Yeah, but what is it?" asked Peter. He rolled off her bed with the book in his hand and started running down the hall. "I'll bet it's love poems for your boyfriends!"

"Peter!" She yelled at him, trying to grab the back of his shirt. "Give it back! It's none of your business."

They were almost to the bathroom door when they heard a sharp knock at the front door. Not too many people came by the apartment at this time of day—almost dinnertime. Peter twirled around, smiling, and held out Elise's private book for her to claim. She snatched it out of his hand without a word.

"I'll get it," he yelled, sounding like he wanted to kick a ball coming his way. The book was forgotten in a moment.

"No, that's all right," came their mother's voice from the front room. She was already there, so Peter and Elise hung in Peter's doorway, listening.

"Mrs. Andersen?" came a man's voice. He sounded out of breath.

"Yes?" Peter's mother seemed a little cautious, as if she didn't recognize the person.

"I'm Per Holrick. I . . . uh . . . I run the women's clothing store down the street?"

"Oh yes." Mrs. Andersen's voice eased up a little. "I've been in your store."

"Good. Well, I'm just going around the neighborhood, letting people know we're going to have a neighborhood all-sing this evening. Just patriotic songs, you know. Not a long time—from six-thirty until people have to go home."

By then Peter's father had come home from work and was padding down the hall in his slippers, pulling on his robe over his office shirt.

"Who's at the door?" he asked as he walked by.

"Mr. Holrick from down the street," Elise explained. "He said there's going to be an all-sing tonight."

But her father had already walked into the front room. Peter and Elise kept listening from Peter's doorway.

"Oh hi, Arne," said the visitor. "I didn't realize you lived here, except for the 'Andersen' sign on the door."

"Holrick," said Mr. Andersen. He sounded as if he knew him from somewhere. "Yes, sure we live here. Same place for ten years! Come in for a cup of tea?"

"Oh, thank you, no. I have to knock on a few more doors to-night. We're just seeing if we can get a few people together from the neighborhood for an all-sing."

"Anyone who hears the voices in the street is sure to come

down, don't you think?" asked Mr. Andersen.

Mr. Holrick laughed nervously. "Sure they will. Unless, of course, they're German. So we'll see you in half an hour?"

"I'll have to see what my wife has planned," replied Peter's father. "I just got home a few minutes ago."

"Fine, then," came the voice from the door. "Good evening to you."

Peter and Elise slipped out into the front room as their mother was latching the front door.

"We're going to go sing, aren't we?" Elise asked expectantly. "We've never been to one of those all-sings."

Peter had seen one once in the street when he was coming home from school. It was one way the Danish people kept their spirits up during the long war, one way they encouraged each other to keep faith.

Mr. Andersen looked at his wife with a worried expression. "It's not just a little sing-along, you know that, dear."

Their mother put her hands on her hips and returned Mr. Andersen's look. "I know that, Arne. But there's usually a street full of people at these all-sings. Don't you think it would be safe enough?"

It surprised Peter that his mother would want to go to such a thing, but he didn't mind. It would be exciting to see who showed up.

"Maybe Grandfather will be there too?" asked Elise hopefully. "He always loves to sing all the old songs." She puffed up her chest, clenched her fists, lowered her voice to a growl, and did her best imitation of Grandfather Andersen. "King Christian stood by the lofty mast, amid the smoke and fog, with his sword—" Her gravelly singing of the familiar song made Peter burst out laughing. Even their father smiled.

"Well, that's a pretty good Grandpa imitation," agreed their mother. "I'm just not sure he'll be out there." She looked sideways at Mr. Andersen. "You two know he hasn't been very well lately, don't you?"

"No, really?" asked Peter. "We didn't know anything about that. Only thing we've noticed is that Grandfather hasn't been down at the boathouse too much the last few weeks. Whenever we go to feed the birds, he's usually not there."

Elise nodded in agreement.

"Well, he's been in and out of the clinic," explained their mother. "And he's been slowing down some. He's just not the type who will complain. All he says is that he's fine, and that he's an old Viking." She shook her head and started toward the kitchen. "Everyone can wash up. Five minutes 'til dinner."

————

After a quick meal (Peter and Elise almost raced each other to see who would finish first), everyone left the dishes on the kitchen table and went to get their heavy coats. Mr. Andersen looked out the window and down the street to see if anyone was gathering yet.

"I can see groups of people heading down the street," he said. "It looks like there may be a crowd." Then he turned to the kids. "Everyone stick together, now. If we get separated for any reason, just get back home here no later than seven."

Peter looked at the clock. Almost six-thirty. This wouldn't be an all-night sing.

"Don't you think we better go?" he asked impatiently.

Mrs. Andersen buttoned up her winter coat and held open the door. "Okay, warm up your singing voices."

Down on the street the early evening chill bit harder than it had during the day. It was still March, after all. No snow had fallen that month, but there was still plenty of slush and ice to slip on. Elise had to hold on to her father's arm to keep from falling.

They were joined by another family heading in the same direction, down the street and around the corner. When they turned the corner, they faced a sea of people, something Peter had never seen before at this time of night. A man had just climbed up on a box and was waving his hands in the air.

"Can everybody hear me?" he yelled. The crowd responded with a chorus of "yesses." People were still streaming in from all directions, and some were even hanging out their apartment windows up and down the street. It was dark, but a few people held candles, sheltering them from the wind. Mostly, the moon lit up the night.

"All right, then, we're going to start with 'Denmark, for a Thousand Years.' Everybody ready?" The man on the soapbox started singing and waving his hands, and it wasn't long before everyone on the street was thundering out the words to the folk song. Peter looked over at his sister singing, sandwiched in between people. As someone pushed in from behind, he grabbed her arm. Already he had lost track of his father.

But the singing—it was almost deafening in the night air. He had never heard a group of people singing so loudly:

"Denmark, for a thousand years, harbors and farms, the free man's birthright . . ."

A man in a big gray overcoat right next to Peter was singing and wiping his eyes at the same time. But that was nothing compared to when they started singing the national anthem, "There Is a Lovely Land."

"Peter!" Elise yelled over the crowd's singing. "We've got to find Mom and Dad!"

Peter looked around, and all he could see were the overcoats of strangers. He nodded and searched for an opening.

"Follow me," he yelled back. Still clinging to Elise's arm, he ducked through a small space between a plump woman and a man in a red mailman's uniform. The man was holding a candle and almost dropped it when Peter and Elise scooted past.

"Excuse me," said Peter, but no one could hear over the crowd. They got to the edge of a building and looked around. All they could make out in the dark were strangers. Lots of singing strangers.

"I think we should just go back home," said Elise, pointing

back in the direction of their apartment.

"Yeah," agreed Peter, "but we don't have a key." He reached into his pocket, just to be sure he didn't have the spare key to the front door. All he felt was a crumpled piece of paper, which he pulled out. He had almost forgotten—the mystery woman's address!

"Hey, Elise." He waved it in front of his sister's face. In the dim light, he could tell she remembered what it was, too. "Now is the perfect time to check it out. It's only a few blocks out of our way."

Peter didn't wait for an answer, but took his sister's hand again and started to thread through the crowd in the direction of the address.

"Peter, what do you suggest we do when we get there?" asked Elise. "Knock on the door and introduce ourselves?"

Peter knew his sister wasn't serious. Still, he wanted her to know that he had at least thought about this.

"You'll see when we get there," he answered mysteriously. Maybe by that time he would have figured something out.

They escaped the crowd and threaded their way down a narrow street. Peter could still hear singing behind them; this time it was "In Denmark I Was Born." It seemed there were hundreds of patriotic Danish songs, and everyone knew every word. There was something that made his spine tingle about the songs. Of course, every Dane alive loved to sing, even on dark city streets in the middle of March during a war. Peter started to hum along.

"Shh!" said Elise. "How much farther?"

Peter looked down at his paper again, clutched tightly in his fist. He couldn't see it, but he remembered the address clearly: South Beach Street, 45-B. He looked up at the row of identical three-story brick apartments and saw a faint glimmer of light coming from under a window shade on the ground floor. 45-B?

"This is it," whispered Peter, but he wasn't quite sure.

"Well, now you know," answered Elise. "Does it look any different than you thought? Let's stop sneaking around and go home before it turns seven."

"No, wait." Peter crossed the street, his mind racing for a way to find out more. "We didn't come all this way just to turn around and go home."

"Yes we did," replied Elise, raising her voice. "Now, come on. We're going to get in big trouble for wandering around like this. And we're not going to visit this Lisbeth von Scriber, or von Schraber—whatever her name is—just because Uncle Morten knew her. Maybe he never even met her. How do we know she's the Lisbeth Dad mentioned?"

Elise twirled on her heel, trying to pull Peter with her. Doing that, she came face-to-face with a young woman walking just behind them. Elise gave a little yelp of surprise.

"Oh, excuse me," she said, letting go of Peter's arm and stepping to the side. "I didn't see—"

The woman behind them had a warm scarf wrapped around her head. Peter thought she looked like a college student—someone young—and she was smiling shyly. She didn't try to walk around Elise.

"Excuse me," said the woman with the scarf. "I don't normally listen in on people's conversations, but I couldn't help overhearing. If you're related to Lisbeth's friend Morten, I'm sure you're welcome at our Bible study. We've been praying especially for Morten."

She smiled again and pointed at the apartment. Peter tried to say something, but his tongue just stuck to the roof of his mouth. All he could do was look over at Elise, hoping she would be able to put her tongue in gear. Now they were found out. But Elise, who usually had something to say, looked about as lively as Peter. Finally she sputtered out something that sounded like "Um, well we need to be getting going . . . I mean, home . . ." Her voice trailed off.

Before they could escape the girl in the scarf, someone had come out the front door of the building and hurried over to where they were having their discussion.

"Don't just stand out here in the cold," said a pretty woman about their Uncle Morten's age. She looked as if she had just stepped out of her living room, which she probably had. "Bring your friends in, Eva. They're welcome to join us."

Eva looked around at Peter and Elise and smiled. "I think we're all coming in, Lisbeth." Then she put her hand on Elise's shoulder, and the three of them followed Lisbeth von Schreider up a couple of steps and into her warm apartment.

"Just for a moment, though," said Elise. "We were really on our way home."

"So did I hear you right when you said Morten is your uncle?" asked Eva as they took off their coats in the hall by the front door. At least a dozen other coats were piled there on chairs and hanging from hooks by the front door.

"Yes, he's our uncle. We were just walking—"

"Oh, I'm sorry, I haven't even introduced myself," said the college girl. "I'm Eva Staffeldt." She turned toward a living room around the corner. "Don't worry. I'll introduce you when we get in."

She didn't need to. Lisbeth peered around the corner just then, a big smile on her face. Her cheeks were rosy from running out into the cold, and her dark, curly hair flowed casually down to her shoulders. "And you two must be Peter and Elise. You look exactly like the photographs your uncle has shown me. I'm Lisbeth von Schreider. I'm a . . . a friend of your Uncle Morten's." She put out her hand for them to shake. "Ooh, your hands are cold! Come on in."

By then Peter was totally confused. Here they were, dragged into some kind of Bible study by people they had never met. They had found this Lisbeth von whatever, and she was smiling at them as if they were old friends. And everyone seemed to know their names already! It wasn't exactly what they had expected, but then, Peter wasn't sure what he had expected when the slip of paper fell out of Uncle Morten's Bible.

The small living room was crowded with about a dozen people, most of them around college age, some a little older; a couple were as old as Uncle Morten and their parents. A few were sitting on the floor, though several of the women had pulled up chairs. They all had Bibles in their laps, and one of the men—probably the leader of the study—was standing to the side.

"I'm sorry to interrupt things again," announced Lisbeth, straightening her hair. She looked at the study leader. "Is this okay, Carlo? Eva ran into some people down on the street that everyone should meet. Everyone, this is Elise and Peter Andersen—Morten's niece and nephew."

They all smiled and nodded as Lisbeth recited their names. Of course Peter had never met any of them before, but he felt welcome in this room full of strangers. When she finished with the introductions, she looked back at the twins.

"I'm so glad you finally came. Morten had always talked so much about you two, about your pigeons and everything. But I have to be nosey—how did you know about this Bible study? Did Morten tell you?"

Elise looked at her brother. "Well, it was Peter's idea, really."

"Oh?" asked Lisbeth.

Peter finally found his tongue. "Well, kind of. We found your name and address on a slip of paper in his Bible, with the note 'Thursdays at seven.'" He pulled out the little wrinkled slip to show her. "We weren't sure what it meant, but we decided to walk by . . . for clues."

Peter snapped his mouth shut. *Why did I spill that last part?* he asked himself. He hadn't meant to go on like that.

Now Lisbeth was smiling again, and Peter wasn't sure why.

"Clues? So you didn't know who this 'Lisbeth von Schreider' was before you came here, did you?" she asked.

"No, but I was . . . we were trying to figure out some ways we could . . . we could maybe get Uncle Morten out of prison," Peter explained. *Stupid again!* He bit his tongue. *Why am I saying all this to these strangers?*

"I mean, everybody here knows about what happened to my uncle, right?" Peter tried to be more cautious this time, glancing around the room. Everyone was listening. Peter wasn't used to having a room full of older people listen to every word he said, and he quickly looked down at the floor. "I know it was a dumb idea. . . ." His voice trailed off.

"Not a dumb idea at all," said the man who was standing up, the man Lisbeth had introduced as Carlo. He was tall and lanky, with a friendly expression, wavy hair, and large, dark glasses. "We've been doing the same thing here at our Bible study ever since Morten was captured. We pretty much know what happened, just not all the details. You probably didn't know that. But"—he waved his hand around the room—"most of us are friends of your uncle. Especially Lisbeth." He winked at her. "We've been doing what we think will work the best to help him, too."

"You guys have a plan?" Peter found himself saying.

"Well, yes, but it may not be what you're thinking. God has the plan. We've been praying every week that He—I mean God—will keep your uncle safe, that He will bring him out of prison, and that He will keep him well, wherever he is."

"Every week?" asked Peter.

"Right here."

Peter had a hard time believing that everyone in this roomful of people was actually praying for his Uncle Morten so often, so close to his home—and he had never known. They had never even met Lisbeth, even though she seemed to talk about Uncle Morten as if he were an old friend.

"Do our mom and dad know?" asked Elise.

"You mean do they know me?" asked Lisbeth, with her easy smile. "Morten and I dated for a few months the summer before last. I did meet your parents, but I'm afraid perhaps they think of me as another one of your uncle's 'religious friends.' And speaking of your parents, aren't they going to be wondering where you two have disappeared to? Did you tell them you were out being detectives?"

"We really are supposed to be getting home," said Elise, a little nervously. "Dad told us that if we got separated at the all-sing, we should meet them at home no later than seven."

Lisbeth looked at her wristwatch and nodded. "The all-sing. I heard about that. Well, it's just five after, so how about if I call your mother and tell her where you are, and that you're on your way home. Is that okay?"

Again Peter and Elise looked at each other, unsure what to say. But Elise nodded. "If you want to," she said.

"What's your phone number?" asked Lisbeth, heading for her small kitchen.

"Bella-three . . ." Suddenly Peter's mind went blank. He could still see the roomful of faces staring right at him. It was like being in school, when the teacher asked him a question in front of everyone. He knew the answer; it was just hiding somewhere.

"Bella-three-seven-six-six," Elise stepped over to tell her, and Lisbeth dialed the number. In a moment, they returned to the group.

"Good thing we called," Lisbeth told Peter. "Your parents were starting to wonder. I told them we found you begging on the street, and that we invited you in, and that you were just leaving. It's a school night, don't forget." Then she took Elise's hand. "Just kidding about the begging part. But I'm glad you two came by. I finally got to meet you. Will you stop by again?"

Elise smiled shyly. "Sure. It's fun to meet Uncle Morten's secret girlfriend."

That made Lisbeth laugh. Peter felt himself feeling more and more comfortable with her as well.

"I'm not so secret," said Lisbeth. "But with a name like von Schreider, maybe I should be." Then her expression turned more serious. "My parents are both from Germany. Sometimes it's hard to prove we're not German spies."

"Maybe you should change your name to Andersen," joked

one of the college students. A few of the girls giggled at the suggestion, and Peter saw Lisbeth's cheeks turn bright red.

"Let's just get Mr. Andersen out of prison first," said the study leader. Then he put down his books. "Tell you what. Since these special guests have to leave, let's set aside our study of John for just a moment and have our prayer time right now. That way, we can pray together again for Morten before Peter and Elise go. Is that okay with everyone? Can we take just a minute?"

As people around the room bowed their heads, Peter got the feeling he had been in the same situation somewhere before. Finally, he remembered. *This is exactly like the night Uncle Morten was captured,* he thought. *Only then Uncle Morten was praying for everybody else—for the Jews who had to escape. Now he needs to escape, and everyone else is praying for him.* For the first time, Peter felt as if they were really doing something to help Uncle Morten.

After they had finished praying, Lisbeth saw them to the door. She stopped for a moment, then turned around quickly and grabbed her own coat off a hook on the wall.

"Carlo, you go ahead without me," she called back into the living room. "I'm going to walk these two back home. I'll just be a few minutes."

"Oh, you don't have to do that," objected Elise.

"No, no, it's fine." Lisbeth opened the door and waited for Peter and Elise. "I don't want you two walking home alone in the dark like this."

Peter started to object too, but by then Lisbeth was walking down the street with them, chatting with Elise like a long-lost sister.

"Oh, you like swing music too?" Elise held on to her new friend's arm as they walked. "A girl I know at school has a bunch of records I've listened to. Richard Johansen's Orchestra—that sort of thing."

"Really?" replied Lisbeth. "My favorite is Svend Asmussen, and—"

"Ooh, he's cute, isn't he?"

Lisbeth giggled a moment. "I've seen his picture. He sure is. How does it go, now?" She puckered up her lips, and her English sounded surprisingly good. " 'It don't mean a thing if it ain't got that swing.' "

The two new friends launched into a spirited chorus of their favorite swing music, ending with the pretend-trombone part.

"Doo-wah, do-wa, doo-wah, do-wa, doo-waah," they sang together, then exploded in a chorus of more giggles. Peter speeded up a couple of steps, hoping that he wouldn't see anyone on the street he knew. Elise looked up from her singing long enough to realize they were almost home.

"We're almost here," she told Lisbeth. "I wish we could have stayed longer."

"Me too," replied Lisbeth. "I'm glad we could meet, even if we do make too much noise for this time of night. I don't think Carlo would have let us sing like that during the Bible study!" She laughed again with Elise while Peter opened their street-level door.

"You're welcome to visit anytime," offered Lisbeth, stopping on the sidewalk. "You too, Peter. Maybe after I get off work sometime."

"Oh, where do you work?" asked Elise.

For a moment Lisbeth seemed flustered. "Oh, I . . . I just work at an office downtown. Paper work kind of thing. But after work . . . you know, before curfew . . . we could put on a couple of my swing records."

"That would be terrific!" said Elise as she turned to go through their front door.

"Just be sure to tell your parents I'm sorry for keeping you two out so late," called Lisbeth.

"Okay, sure!" Elise called back. "We'll tell them, and we'll see you again." She climbed the stairs two at a time as Peter shut the door behind them.

"She's sure nice, isn't she?" bubbled Elise. "I'm glad Uncle Morten likes her."

Peter didn't say anything, just followed Elise up the stairs. "Yeah, but Uncle Morten sure can't listen to her records where he is right now," he muttered.

"What did you say?" asked Elise brightly.

"Nothing," replied Peter, scuffling up the last few stairs. "Nothing at all."

UNDERGROUND PRINTERS

The air raid came early during the first class period, even before Peter's teacher, Mrs. Bernsted, had finished with the roll call. As usual, the wail of the sirens made Peter jump, and he knocked his books all over the floor.

"Please bring your spelling and math lessons with you to the shelter," called out Mrs. Bernsted. She had to shout to be heard above the sirens, but the class was used to it by now. After all, they had been through nearly five years of the routine. It was just coming more and more often lately, with British planes flying overhead almost every day. While Peter gathered his things off the floor, the rest of the class lined up at the door. Mrs. Bernsted shot Peter an impatient glance.

"Are you ready, Peter? Time to go."

"Coming," Peter shouted. He stuffed all his papers back into his little desk, grabbed his book, and hurried to the end of the line as people started to leave. It would be better when they got downstairs into the school's basement. Not so loud.

It *was* better, but Peter still had trouble concentrating on the day's math problems. He had always had trouble with fractions anyway. At the top of his paper, where it should have said "Math," Peter wrote, "Action Plan to Free Uncle Morten." Then he started to make his list.

First, there was "Find out for sure where he's at." They weren't positive that he was still in Vestre Prison. He could ask again at the newspaper if someone could find out. Number two was "Find a car or something to drive." Of course, they would have to find a driver. This was getting a little more complicated. He scratched his head with the end of his pencil. Well, number three? He almost had to laugh, now that he thought about it. Elise was right. This was about the silliest thing he had ever come up with. To think that they could actually drive up to a German prison and—

Peter's thoughts were interrupted by someone snickering behind him. Peter covered his paper with his hand and glanced around just in time to see Keld Poulsen slipping back into his seat. Had he seen? With the smirk on Keld's face, Peter didn't have to guess. Peter wadded up the paper he was writing on and shoved it in his pocket. He wished he could keep his ears from turning beet red, but sometimes he just couldn't help it.

"Are you having trouble, Peter?" Mrs. Bernsted looked over to see how many math problems he had worked.

"No, Mrs. Bernsted, no problem." Peter turned the page in his workbook and scribbled down a quick answer to $^{11}/_{17}$ minus $^5/_{34}$. He felt as if his ears were still steaming with embarrassment. Why didn't the teacher catch Keld spying over Peter's shoulder?

"Then please don't waste any more paper," she commanded. "We certainly don't have enough to waste."

"Yes, ma'am." Peter went back to his math problems, until the boy in front of him passed back a note.

"Hey, Peter," a boy named Finn Dahl had scribbled at the top. Peter played with him outside sometimes, but mostly they drew pictures together. "Guess which one."

Peter and Finn had played this game before. Finn would draw a picture of an airplane, and Peter would guess what kind it was.

British Mosquito bombers, American P–51 fighters; each had their own distinctive wings and engines. Peter and Finn could probably recognize the real thing from far off if they ever saw one. This time, Finn had drawn the distinctive cigar-shaped twin engines of the British Mosquito, with the pointed nose in the middle. Even though the drawing was small, Peter was quite sure.

"Mosquito," he printed at the top of the paper and passed it toward Finn with a grin. As he did, Peter caught a glimpse of someone brushing up next to them from behind. Keld again.

"Here," whispered Keld. "I'll take that." He reached out and snatched the drawing from Peter's hand before Finn could take it.

"Hey, get your own," Finn protested in his high voice. Mrs. Bernsted looked up with an annoyed expression.

"Would you boys please settle down?" she told them, the irritation coming through. "I don't want to have to tell you again."

"I was just turning in Finn's paper for him," said Keld in the pretend-innocent voice he often used for getting other people into trouble. He walked over to the teacher and handed her the airplane drawing, then returned to his seat with a smirk.

Mrs. Bernsted studied the paper for a moment, and Peter thought he saw a tiny hint of a smile. But when Mrs. Bernsted spoke, she was stern once more.

"That's a very nice drawing, Finn." A couple of girls twittered in the back row, and Anette Steving in the front row turned around to gloat. *She always does that when we're in trouble,* fumed Peter.

"However," continued the teacher, "this is not art class. Since it seems that you three boys have nothing better to do during math period, you will all do an additional page of word problems, to be handed in before you leave for home today. Page one thirty-four. Do you understand?"

Peter and Finn nodded, and Peter heard Keld groan behind him.

"You're in real trouble now, Andersen," Keld whispered at

him when the room was quiet. Peter tried to ignore him as he
opened his math book again.

———————

On the way home from school that day Peter told Elise what
had happened with Keld in the air-raid shelter. His sister twisted
her hair as she listened and made a face.

"Ooh, that Keld Poulsen makes me so mad!" she fumed, shifting a pile of books from one arm to the other. "I don't understand
why he's always after you like that. One of these days I'm just
going to walk right up to him and punch him out!" Elise made a
fist, and Peter had to smile.

"The thing I don't get is that he acts like some kind of Nazi,
like he hates me because of what we're doing. He even got mad
at me when it was his fault for picking up Finn's drawing and
giving it to Mrs. Bernsted."

"Drawing?" asked Elise. "What were you two drawing? I
thought you said it was math period."

"I know I said that. But, it's just something Finn and I do
sometimes. He likes to draw airplanes and have me figure out
what kind they are. He's not very good at sports, but he's a great
artist."

"I know." Elise rolled her eyes. "He's kind of the professor
type, right? So you have the professor in front of you and the
bully in back of you, and Peter in the middle is always getting
into trouble."

Peter looked behind him as they walked away from the big
brick school building. "Well, speaking of the bully, he's probably
following us right now. He does that a lot. Says he's going to get
me."

"But he never has yet." Elise followed her brother's glance,
searching the crowds of kids. Some were just getting on the bicycles they had left leaning on the school's wooden rack. Others,
like them, were walking down the bumpy streets on their way
home, dodging bikes and a few odd trucks. For March, it was still

cold, and everyone looked like little locomotives blowing off steam.

"I don't see him," she added, glancing back at Peter. "Maybe we just need to watch out for him."

"Right. He already knows we deliver Underground papers. Think he would tell anyone?"

"Maybe. Race you."

The twins ran as fast as they could around the block, cut through an alley, and then took a roundabout way to the back door of the dentist's office where *The Free Dane* was published. Peter looked back once more and saw nothing. Finally, he could breathe a little easier, at least after he caught his breath from running. They slipped inside.

Behind what looked like a closet door was a flight of stairs leading down to a furnace room. But there was one more door, and before Peter knocked, Elise put her hand on his shoulder.

"I already told them everything," she said to Peter.

"About what?"

"About what happened at the dry cleaners. Bent saw me on the street the next day, so he already knows. I think somebody else told him too, because he didn't seem surprised."

Peter nodded. "Then we don't have to explain everything all over again?"

"No."

Peter nodded again and knocked lightly three times, then twice, and finally once more. It was their prearranged signal, and a moment later Peter heard a muffled voice behind the door.

"Yes?" came a squeaky teenaged voice.

"Christian and Margrete here," replied Elise. From the first day, they were strictly told not to use anyone's real names. In fact, no one in the newspaper knew anyone's real names, in case they ever were made to tell. Elise had come up with Christian (a name used by Danish kings) and Peter had suggested Margrete (the name of the only Danish queen back in the 1300s).

A small, dark-haired boy wearing an ink-stained apron

peeked out from around the door. He was barely five years older than Peter and Elise, and he was the newspaper's all-around errand boy. He smiled when he saw them and pulled the door back farther.

"Hey, your majesties."

"Hi, Bent," said Peter, using the only name the twins knew for the boy. "We—"

"You're back," interrupted Bent. Even though Elise had already told him about the dry cleaners, he acted as if nothing had happened. Then he flashed them another grin and wiped his inky hands on his apron. "I was starting to wonder."

Without another word he stepped back into the shadows. Peter and Elise followed, closing and locking the door carefully behind them. They entered a dark basement room, filled with the strong tea smell of ink and the clackety-clack sound of a small printing press. This was the office, production center, and newsroom for *The Free Dane*, one of dozens of Underground newspapers scattered throughout Denmark. They operated in basements and attics, printing the real news about what was happening in their country and across Europe during the war.

Two other men sat sharing one small lamp at a table next to the printing press. One whom Peter had never seen before was composing a story on an ancient Remington typewriter; the other was scribbling something by hand. Neither of them looked up.

The press itself, run by a third man, was a rattling machine cast off by a local printshop years ago. Peter thought it might have been as old as printing itself—the year "1890" was stamped on the side. The man tending the press, an older fellow with graying hair, looked up and grunted.

"Hey, kids," he shouted between the clank-plunk rhythm of the press. "Glad to see you. I'll just be about another ten minutes, and then we'll have something for you to take out. We've missed you the last couple of days, but I heard what happened at the dry cleaners."

Peter nodded, while Elise went to look over the shoulder of

the man at the typewriter. Peter shuffled over to the press, keeping time with the thump of the machine. The silver-haired fellow—or Kaspar, as they called him—may have been the "old man" of the newspaper staff, but he could keep the printing press cranking better than anyone else. He looked over at Peter.

"Here, ready to take over? Give the old man a break?" he asked.

"Sure!" Peter was glad for the chance to do something, and he had never actually had his hand on the press before. This was usually the apprentice's job.

"Just watch it. Keep your fingers away, but make sure there's enough paper in the tray there," warned the pressman. "Keep an eye on the paper feed, keep it cranked up, and make sure they all go in smoothly. Got it?"

"No problem." Peter tried to look as if he understood everything the man had said, but just then one of the papers jammed. There was a racket of flapping paper before Kaspar reached over and flipped off a red switch.

"I didn't do it!" Peter said as he threw up his hands.

Kaspar only chuckled and scratched his nose, leaving a black streak. He reached in to yank out a scrap of paper that had wedged itself between two rollers. "No one's blaming you. It's just this old antique and this scrap paper we have to print on. Here, see? Could be a lot worse."

The typing over at the other side of the room paused, and Peter looked over to see the man staring suspiciously at Peter and Elise. It looked like the first time he had noticed them.

"Where did you get the kids, Kaspar?" asked the typist. He picked up a pencil and tapped it nervously on the typewriter in front of him.

"Kids?" replied the older man. "Oh, you mean Chris and Grete? They're two of the best carriers we have."

"Sure, but—" The typist wasn't convinced.

"Listen, Victor," continued the pressman. "These are good

kids. I know their uncle. And besides, they sort of walked into the job."

"How's that?" Peter was sure that this Victor, the typist, was one of the sourest characters he had seen in a long time.

"Well . . ." Kaspar drew up his belt and leaned against his press. "I was delivering these things myself last year, and we weren't getting anything done."

"Which is why we brought Bent in here," said Victor.

"Yes, of course. But let me tell you, since you asked. As I said, I was delivering these things myself to the railroad station last year, right around Christmastime, and I left a bundle on one of the station benches for people to pick up. Then I strolled back here to the dentist's office."

Kaspar pointed to the twins, who were standing awkwardly next to him. "These two saw me in the station, and they followed me here through all the crowds."

Peter wasn't sure he liked Kaspar telling the story to Victor, but of course he couldn't interrupt him. The cranky typist had his chin in his hands and his elbows on the table in front of him. At least he was listening. So was the other man at the table, a quieter fellow named Rudy.

"So I get here to the shop," continued Kaspar, "and I discover I have these two shadows. Both of them are holding a paper, and they look up at me with these big puppy eyes as I'm standing there." He waved toward the door.

"They're cold, they're breathing hard, and both of them ask me if they can help deliver our newspaper," he continued. "They tell me they want to help do something because their uncle is part of the Underground. So you tell me, Victor, what am I supposed to say? I need the help. You need the help. They want to help. And they do a fine job."

"Hmmph." Victor wasn't frowning as much after the story, but Peter still wasn't convinced that he thought much of the twins. Then the man went back to his typing.

"Don't mind him," Kaspar told Peter and Elise. "He's always

a grouch. That's the way a lot of those big-city reporters are. Come here, Chris, and I'll get you going on this press. I have to get a few things."

Peter was used to being called his code name by now. He took his place next to the press, while Kaspar started the ancient machine once more. It started up slowly, like a dinosaur coming to life. Then it slipped into its peculiar clackety rhythm once more while Kaspar disappeared into another room.

"Hey, Elise," Peter called over to his sister. "Look at me!"

Elise had moved to look over the shoulder of the other man writing at the table. She glanced up long enough to give him a thumbs-up signal, then looked away again. No one else heard that Peter had used Elise's real name, and Peter breathed a quiet sigh of relief. After a couple of minutes watching the press, Peter started looking at the papers slipping out one at a time, trying to read them as they piled up.

"The usual war news," explained the man next to Elise, the one named Rudy. He was a stocky man with curly brown hair, younger than their parents. Peter had never seen him get out of his chair, so he wasn't sure how tall he was. Rudy was usually nice to the twins. "The Germans are on the run," he said between his teeth. "But of course you won't read that anywhere else."

Peter tried to read one of the stories at the top of the page, something about a building in Aarhus being blown up. Finally he slipped his fingers in and grabbed one of the printed papers as it came off the press, being careful not to upset the pile. A small sketch of a person waving a Danish flag caught his eye.

"Hey, that drawing's pretty good," remarked Peter, studying it. Something looked vaguely familiar about it, but he guessed he had probably just seen something else by the same artist in the paper before. "Did one of you do it?"

"Wish I had," replied Rudy. "Someone slips them under the door once every few weeks. No name. But the old man likes them, so we run them." He paused long enough to jerk his thumb in the direction Kaspar had disappeared. A moment later, the old printer returned with a small can of black ink.

"Someone mention my name?" asked Kaspar, prying the top of the ink can off with a screwdriver.

"We were just talking about the mystery artist," shouted Peter over the clatter of the press. "You really don't know who it is?"

"What's that?" The older man came in and shut down the machine. It left Peter's ears ringing.

"The mystery artist," Peter repeated. "You don't know who it is?"

"Oh that," replied the man. "No, I don't. Not a clue. There's never any name on the things." He took a putty knife and slathered a scoop of gooey black ink into a cup on the side of the press. "But the drawings just keep coming, and they're very good. Mostly city scenes, everyday stuff, but everybody loves them." After packing the ink down like honey in a jar, he checked the paper once more and started the machine back up. Then he patted Peter on the back.

"Thanks for watching the press. Not bad for your first time," yelled Kaspar. "Maybe I should have you come by and do this more often. Bent starts out good, but he gets bored."

"I didn't do anything, really." Peter shrugged and stepped out of the way, all the time keeping his eyes on the papers coming out. "Just stood here and watched them come out." He counted down from ninety-nine, trying to keep up the pace. Eighty, then seventy. Finally twenty-five. Then ten, nine, eight . . .

Kaspar grinned and wiped his brow with the only part of his hand that wasn't covered with black ink. "Well, you do a fine job at that. If you ever want to change your career, let me know."

"You mean you need more slave labor," said Victor sourly.

"Did we ask you?" replied the old man. The typist looked as if he were used to that kind of teasing. Kaspar picked up another stack of paper, loaded it into the feeder of the printing press, and adjusted a small knob on the side. Then he turned to Peter and Elise once more.

"See, it's like I told you. Reporters are all alike, even reporters for Underground newspapers. Cynical, every one of them."

"Cynical?" asked Peter.

"You know," explained Kaspar. "Someone who always sees the worst in things. People who don't like art, probably not even the drawings that we run."

"On the contrary," said Victor. He finally stopped typing and leaned back in his chair. Then he pushed his hat back from his forehead and ran his fingers through a thin lock of blond hair. "Aside from the writing, they're the best little thing in the paper." He flashed a rare grin with his dark, coffee-stained teeth.

"Well, what do you know?" said Kaspar to the twins. "I think that's probably the first decent thing I've heard that man say yet." He ducked as the typist threw a crumpled wad of paper at his head. "I've certainly heard him say worse things." Peter and Elise laughed. The men at the Underground newspaper sometimes talked tough, but mostly they acted like big kids.

"Speaking of the worst of things, does anybody know what happened to Mr. Sundberg? The dry cleaner?" Peter had meant to ask earlier but was afraid of what he might learn.

"He's back home," Victor mumbled. Peter wondered how he could carry on a conversation, scowl, type, and chew gum all at the same time.

"Yeah," chimed in Bent. He had just returned from a back room. "You two really lucked out. So did Sundberg. Germans couldn't find anything in his shop, but they tore it apart trying. Busted a few windows. He was completely clean, though. A customer had grabbed his papers and walked out with them just in time. Good thing. And in case you're wondering, we're not going to have you drop there anymore."

"So where do we take them now?" asked Elise. She looked at Bent, who was their usual contact for dropping off and picking up their newspapers.

"Tailor, two blocks down from the cleaners and around the corner," answered Bent. "You know it?"

Peter thought for a moment, trying to imagine the street.

There was the candy store, a bank, a doctor's office, and, yes, a small tailor's shop. He had never been inside, just walked by.

"Oh yeah," said Peter. "I know where it is. Tiny little place, right? Like for men's clothes?"

"That's it," replied the teenager. "Jorgensen's. You can use the same shirts you used for the cleaners to pack the papers in. And we'd like to give you a few more drop-off spots, too. Maybe even have you distribute to the buses. One of the other delivery kids just quit. Okay with you?"

Peter looked over at his sister and gulped. "Sure, I guess so. Right, Grete?"

Elise wrinkled her eyebrows, but she nodded slowly. "Okay."

"Well, we can start you with your first load right now," said Kaspar. "It's still a little wet, but isn't it always?"

Peter took a copy of the little newspaper and blew on it to keep the ink from smudging in his hand. A few minutes later, Peter and Elise each had a larger bundle than usual, all tucked into their brown paper packages of shirts.

"Come on, Grete," he said. "Let's go see if it's clear out back before we leave."

Alone again, Peter and Elise peeked out the door. It looked clear, and Keld Poulsen was nowhere in sight. Before he closed the door, though, Peter heard the two men at the table mumbling something, then arguing.

Elise tugged at Peter's sleeve with her free hand. "Come on, while it's clear," she whispered.

"Wait a minute," Peter whispered back. "You think they're arguing about us? What are they upset about?" Peter pointed back with his thumb, where the men were getting louder.

"It's not right, I tell you," said the curly-haired reporter. "People are going to get hurt. I mean killed."

"No they're not," replied Victor. He always sounded so sure of himself. "At least not any of our people. We've been begging London to bomb the Shell House for months, and now they finally say maybe, and you're worried?"

The Shell House! Peter had heard about the place. It was a big office building in Copenhagen, taken over by the Germans as a special headquarters. Bent had told them that to protect themselves, the Germans had built a small prison on the top floor and filled it with captured Danish Resistance workers. Peter had wondered if Uncle Morten was being held there.

"Of course I'm worried," replied Rudy. "I know guys who are probably in that prison, guys who—"

"I told you, they're going to precision-bomb just the lower floors. We've sent the Brits building plans, maps, everything. Just the bottom floors, not the top floors. They'll lob those bombs in there like soccer balls into the goal. None of the good guys are going to get hurt if everything goes right."

"If. If. That's a big risk to take."

"Bigger not to take. They're putting together records there that will shut down just about every Resistance work in Denmark. We have to take it out, and that's all there is to it. Latest word is it's going to happen sometime before the month is out. But you keep that quiet."

Peter and Elise didn't wait around to hear any more. In a moment, they were out the door, down the alley, and out on the street.

"Wow," said Peter. "Did you hear that? A bombing raid!"

"Sure, but it's way down in Copenhagen. Good thing it's not here." Then Elise held Peter back for a moment by the sleeve, and she looked straight at him. There were times when Peter was sure she could read his mind. Maybe it had something to do with being twins. "We don't know that Uncle Morten is there, Peter."

"But do we know he's not? Come on, let's find the tailor's and get rid of these shirts."

They started to jog through the crowded streets on their way to the tailor's shop, and Peter thought about his uncle again. *Could he be in the Shell House? What if he's there when it's bombed? Will the British really only bomb the lower floors? What if they miss?*

They were almost to the shop when Elise steered Peter right

where they should have gone left.

"What are you doing, Elise?" protested Peter. "The shop is the other way." He tried to turn back, but Elise put her arm around his shoulder and pulled him back.

"Knock it off, Peter," she hissed at him. She was trying to talk without looking like she was talking, and Peter had a hard time understanding her.

"What?" said Peter, wondering what had gotten into his sister. "What are you talking about?"

"We just passed your friend Keld Poulsen back there, leaning against a building. That's what I'm talking about."

Peter started to turn his head. "You think he's going to follow us?"

Elise pinched Peter in the back of the neck to keep his head from turning.

"Don't look now," she whispered. "Let's just go faster and double back. See if he's really following us."

The late afternoon streets were filled with people on their way home from work. It wasn't hard for Peter and Elise to quicken their pace, jog a little, and turn a corner. As soon as they did, Peter spied a little butcher shop on the corner.

"Quick," he said, taking Elise's arm. "In here."

They slipped into the little shop, closing the door quickly behind them. The pleasant jingle of bells on the door made the plump butcher behind the counter look up. He was with a customer, and there were three or four other people waiting in the small store.

"Be right with you after I take care of these people," he said and returned to the woman who was in front of the counter.

Peter said nothing, just slipped up to the front of the line with Elise and pretended to look at the sausages behind the glass case. The woman they were now in front of cleared her throat impatiently.

"Excuse me, children," said the woman. She was about their grandfather's age and sounded quite ready to put Peter and Elise out on the street. Elise turned to her and smiled.

"I'm so sorry, ma'am," said Elise. "We're not here to buy any-thing. Just looking. We have to leave in a minute."

"Well!" huffed the woman.

Peter scooted in a little closer behind the old woman and smiled too. Then he ducked down to examine the meat case, and looked upside down under his arm out at the street. It wasn't a moment before Keld came tearing around the corner, followed by a German officer in a gray uniform. Both of them stopped and looked down the street, then back the other way. The officer seemed familiar to Peter.

"Do you recognize the man with Keld?" Peter asked his sister. She was peering out at the street too from behind the old woman. The woman turned and glared at the twins, then she began to stare out the window with them.

"Don't you remember?" asked Elise. "That's the guy who was there the time Henrik broke his arm. The German officer who's always snooping around down by the harbor."

Then Peter remembered the steely, evil-sounding man—the one with a crooked nose who looked like a prizefighter. He re-membered the time when his friend Henrik had broken his arm down by Grandfather's fishing boat. They had tumbled down the dock ramp and almost rolled right into the German officer.

"I remember now. Major something." Peter had a sinking feel-ing that he would have to meet this man again sometime. He ducked back behind the old woman.

"Look," whispered Elise. "Your major is talking with Keld."

Peter peeked again. Actually, the officer's finger was in Keld's face, as if the man were giving Keld a good lecture. The young bully seemed to melt before the German, and he looked scared. Then Keld pointed off down the street, and they both continued in the direction they had been going.

"Young man," snapped the old woman. "Whoever you're playing hide-and-seek with, you're going to have to move out of the line now. We're here for our dinner sausage, if there's any left in this city to eat."

"Yes, I'm sorry," Peter apologized. Then he turned back to the butcher, who had finished serving the customer at the head of the line. "Thanks."

He and Elise shuffled to the front of the store and peeked carefully out the door. Keld and the German were just disappearing around the next corner, heading in the opposite direction of the tailor's shop.

"We're going to have to stay away from that guy, no matter what," said Elise.

"That's what I've always said," agreed Peter, and he skipped out ahead of her.

The tailor's shop wasn't hard to find, but Peter stopped before they went in together.

"What if this isn't the right place?" he worried.

"Not the right place?" Elise urged him on through the door. "What are you talking about?"

The door jingled as they walked in, and a middle-aged man with a pair of scissors in his hand looked up from behind a bolt of black cloth. Everywhere else around the shop were small racks of shirts and suits, neatly arranged by size. Several mannequins stood at the end of each aisle of clothes, each wearing half-sewn gray suit jackets. The man smiled at them with a mouthful of sewing pins between his lips.

"Can I help you?" he asked, pulling the pins out.

Peter and Elise looked at each other for a second, wondering who would say something first. Finally Elise cleared her throat.

"We're supposed to drop these shirts by for you," she said, her voice quivering only a little. Peter wasn't sure why they were both so nervous; they were the only ones in the little shop. The man gave them a quizzical look.

"Was this for an alteration?" he asked. "A repair, perhaps?"

"No," answered Elise. "Bent sent them."

"Bent, Bent," the man repeated, his face still blank. He pulled a measuring tape from his pocket. Then his face lit up.

"Oh, Bent. Shirts. Yes, yes, of course, I'm sorry." The little man rushed forward from behind his material. He wasn't much taller than Elise. "I'm sorry to keep you guessing. It's just that I've never done this sort of thing before." He took the two packages from Peter and Elise and disappeared with them into a back room. By that time, a girl had come in from the street and was waiting by the counter. When the little man reappeared, he turned once more to the twins.

"Now, come back tomorrow, and I'll have them all repaired for you," he said, dismissing them. "You'll have some pants to alter?"

Peter and Elise nodded, said goodbye, and turned out to the street.

"Well, that wasn't so hard," Elise told her brother as they headed home. "We just have to make sure we don't run into your school buddy again."

LAST WARNING

For the next week, Peter stayed as far away from Keld Poulsen as he possibly could. At school, he tried to wait until the other boy got into line, and then put as many people as he could between them. When he had to pass papers back down the row, he didn't look back, just held the stack over his shoulder and waited for the other boy to take them. It wasn't always easy, but Peter managed to stay out of Keld's way pretty well.

After school Friday, Peter and Elise rushed to collect their papers at the back of the dentist's office. They didn't stay around to chatter with Bent, only looked both ways down the alley and rushed off for their first drop-off with the little tailor. They ran back and forth that way for three more loads, each time without any problems. All that time, they never ran into Keld on the street—never even saw him. After an hour, midafternoon started turning dark once more. The dark Danish winter was still hanging on.

"You know," Peter observed as they were returning home after their last load. "Keld hasn't beat me up like I thought he would the other day. In fact, I've hardly seen him. He hasn't said a word to me."

"Really?" asked Elise. She stopped to look into a shop window—a record store with a display of a phonograph player. Someone had set a little stuffed white dog in the window, and it was looking at the big funnel of the player, just like the advertisements for that kind of American record. "So maybe we're in the clear with that old bully. Maybe he's got better things to do than pester the Andersen twins. Besides—"

Elise spun around with her fists in the air in front of her and challenged Peter to shadowboxing.

"Besides," she said. "He wouldn't dare try to beat up on my little brother. Not with me around."

Peter put up his hands, palms out, and laughed while Elise play-boxed. He liked it when his sister acted this silly, which wasn't often. Most of the time, she was the one telling him to settle down.

"Elise Andersen, prizefighter and next winner of the ultra-flyweight class world boxing title." They both laughed as Peter shuffled and ducked. But a moment later, the sparkle in Elise's eyes blinked off, and she put her hands down limply. She stood there looking over Peter's shoulder.

"Come on, champ," Peter urged her. He stuck out his chin and pointed to it. "Free shot. Come on, I dare you. Free shot."

"Peter," she said, crossing her arms defensively. "Turn around."

The smile left Peter's face as quickly as his sister's had when he turned around to face Keld Poulsen. The boy was standing two paces from Peter, his arms crossed to match Elise's.

"Oh, it's you," said Peter, his voice barely making it out of his throat.

"So, Andersen." The big boy tossed a coin up and down in his hand. "Out playing newspaper boy again? Or is it professional boxer today?" He looked over at Elise and half smiled. He was not trying to be pleasant.

"Oh, excuse me, please," continued Keld. "Make that news-paper boy and girl. You're both helping the cause, aren't you?"

Peter felt his blood almost boil as the older boy taunted them, but his feet seemed glued to the sidewalk. Elise tapped him on the shoulder.

"Come on, Peter," she whispered at him. "Let's go."

Peter was about to turn and follow his sister, but Keld stepped forward and grabbed Peter's coat. One of the front buttons popped off and rolled into the gutter.

"Hey, you leave my brother alone!" Elise objected.

"Back off!" sneered Keld, hanging on to Peter's coat. He picked Peter off his feet and used him as a bumper to hit Elise. Peter knew he could try to club the boy, but Keld's bulk was over-powering. He felt like a fish on a hook.

"Listen, I've just come to give you a message," continued Keld. His nose was running from the cold, so he lowered his face and wiped it on Peter's sleeve. "It's from a friend of mine who knows all about these rinky-dink newspapers. The kind of junk you guys pass out."

"What's wrong with those little newspapers?" Peter found himself saying. He looked straight into Keld's eyes. Finally the bully shook his head in disgust and shoved Peter down hard. Peter fell on his back, and Elise tried to catch her brother, but they both ended up sprawling on the sidewalk. Keld laughed and slapped his knee.

"What's wrong with those little newspapers?" Keld mimicked Peter's question in a high, squeaky voice. "What's wrong is that they're stupid, and they're against the law, or maybe you didn't know—"

"Against whose law? Nazi laws?" Elise interrupted, getting to her feet. Peter could see the fire in her eyes, but he didn't want his sister to get hurt. He wished someone they knew would come by on the street, someone who would get them out of this mess. Instead, most people didn't seem to notice and walked right on by.

"Oh, you're a real tough sister, aren't you?" Keld wasn't through with his taunting, and he stepped up to Elise's challenge. "Well, when my friends find out what you're doing, they're going to come in and tear your little pretend newspaper apart, piece by piece."

"You're sick, Keld," said Peter, brushing himself off. He didn't feel the same anger he had before. Now he only felt sorry for the bully, maybe even a little bit of disgust. Really sorry, when he thought of the kind of "friends" Keld was talking about—the kind of friends who wore Nazi uniforms.

"And you're stupid," retorted Keld. "Want some advice?"

"No," replied Elise. "But you're probably going to give it to us anyway."

"For once, you're right. If you don't want to get into big trouble, you better knock off the newspaper-boy stuff. Because we'll follow you, and we'll find you."

"Thanks for the kind warning," said Elise. "We'll be sure to think about it."

Keld wagged his chubby finger at them. "I'm just warning you, okay? I didn't have to do this. But it's the last time."

Elise wasn't listening anymore. She turned her back on Keld and took Peter's arm. Her brother was just picking up his lost button out of the gutter and stuffing it into his pocket. "Come on, Peter. He doesn't have anything else to say."

The twins didn't look back, and Peter did his best to keep looking straight ahead as he walked.

"Don't run," Elise whispered out the side of her mouth.

Peter knew that if his sister hadn't said that, he would have been flying down the street. Instead, they walked straight ahead, flat-footed, straining to hear footsteps following them. Peter knew they could outrun Keld easily if they had to. Elise didn't say anything else all the way home—only muttered under her breath.

TRADING SECRETS

"Peter! Hold it a minute!"

Peter's grandfather waved as he ambled toward the boat-house.

"Afternoon, Grandpa." Peter was heading out the door but changed his mind. As usual, it was overcast outside, and cold enough to remind him that it wasn't spring yet.

"I haven't seen you or your sister here at the boathouse too much lately," wheezed Grandfather Andersen as he came through the door. "You just feed the pigeons and run."

"We still take them out and fly them some."

"Really?" Grandfather Andersen leaned against his work-bench and coughed. "When was the last time?"

Peter couldn't actually remember. Maybe it had been a few weeks ago ... maybe even before Christmas. He scratched his head. "I guess I don't remember, Grandpa. We've been pretty busy with school and everything."

His grandfather nodded again and coughed some more. Peter frowned, squinted, and took a few steps closer.

"Mom said you've been to the clinic, Grandpa."

"Humph!" His grandfather walked stiffly over to the pigeon coop part of the shed and whistled at one of the birds, who fluttered off to a corner. "Just a checkup. It's going to take a lot more than that to slow down an old Viking like me."

"Mom said it was something about your lungs?"

"Don't let her worry you any. I'm fine. In fact, we should all get some poles and go out fishing this afternoon."

Peter looked around the shed. He hadn't been fishing with his grandfather since he was a little boy. "Really? Today? Out in the cold?"

"Cold, nothing! I may not have a boat anymore, but we can still catch us a few bottom fish here off the pier, don't you think? They're not bad to eat, with a little extra sauce. Go get your sister."

Peter didn't need any more convincing. *Maybe if we catch a few fish,* he thought, *we can give them to Mom to cook up for dinner.*

When the twins returned, out of breath from running the whole way, Grandfather Andersen was already out the door with three old fishing poles over his shoulder. Peter ran up beside him and took an ancient toolbox from his hand.

"What's in here?" asked Peter.

"Just a few old hooks. Fishing line. That sort of thing."

"What are we using for bait?" asked Elise. She didn't have anything to carry, so Grandfather gave her one of the poles.

"Eggs," replied their grandfather. "Fish eggs. I got them from a friend, and I thought we'd better use them before they went bad."

"That's a good excuse for fishing," said Peter. Even though it was cold and there was no one else on the pier except an occasional sea gull, it felt good to be outside. In fact, it was warmer than it had been all month. When they found a spot at the end of the pier, everyone untangled the lines, baited their hooks with little purple-red fish eggs that Grandfather pulled from an old tin can, and slowly dropped their lines in the water. Grandfather Andersen looked down at his line and started to laugh.

"What's so funny?" asked Elise.

"Oh, it's not so funny," answered her grandfather. "It's just that I'm not used to catching fish this way—one at a time. I haven't done it without a net for a long time."

"Really?" asked Peter. "So why now?"

"Well, how else can I spend any time with my grandchildren?" He smiled and pulled his line to check on the bait. "But I can still remember how to do this, you see?" His bait was already gone, and as he tried to bait the hook once more, he started into one more of his coughing spells. Peter patted him on the back, wondering what to do for him.

"Are you okay?" asked Elise when her grandfather's coughing had slowed down.

"It's just a little tickle in the throat," he wheezed. "Can't get it out."

"Sounds like more than a tickle," observed Elise. She scrunched up her face and looked at her grandfather with wrinkled eyebrows.

"So!" Grandfather Andersen threw his line out again. "We're not here to talk about my little coughs. Tell me what you two have been doing lately. You don't play down at the boathouse anymore . . . not since Henrik had to leave. You're both always so serious, like the world is depending on you. I don't see your friends around. Don't you do anything for fun anymore?"

"We do fun stuff, Grandpa," answered Peter. "We're fishing, aren't we?"

"Yes, but this was my idea. I mean, really. Are you already two adults that don't play? You're way too serious. It's just run down to the boathouse, feed the birds, and run out. I can't ever catch you anymore. Do you even still play with dolls, Elise?"

Elise laughed for a moment. "Sometimes with the girls at school, Grandpa. And we play things at recess. You know, ball and that sort of thing. We're not totally serious."

"Oh, I'm sure you do." Grandfather tried to tickle Peter in the ribs, and Peter had to giggle.

"Cut it out, Grandpa," Peter protested. "I'm too—"

"Oh, that's right. I forgot. You're too old for tickling." Grand-father gave Peter an extra tickle for good measure. "Well, I suppose that's all right. But I'm talking about *after* school. What are you two so busy with after school?" He looked straight into Peter's eyes, with the warm sort of look that Peter couldn't escape.

Now, more than anything, Peter wanted to tell him all about their working with the Underground newspaper. Somebody had to know. Instead, Peter busied himself with pulling in his line and checking the bait.

"Oh, I don't know," replied Peter uneasily. "We run errands and stuff." He kept his eyes out on the water, where a faint ghost of a sun was trying to break through the clouds. With no wind that afternoon, the water lay calm and untroubled. Peter liked it that way. He watched one of the big ferries that shuttled back and forth to Sweden start to pull out of the harbor, followed by a tug-boat. Behind the two boats came long, spreading wakes, and then the swells disappeared underneath the pier. Peter hoped the boats wouldn't scare their fish away.

"Okay, I'll tell you what," offered their grandfather. "We can trade secrets. One for one. If you have anything to share, I'll trade you for something about me. Is that a deal?"

Elise smiled at her grandfather. "Deal," she said. "But we get to ask the first question."

Grandfather rolled his eyes and grinned. "Okay, fire when ready."

Elise turned to her brother. "What should we ask him? Now's our chance."

"I know," said Peter. "Have you ever done anything against the law, Grandfather? Something illegal?"

"Peter!" scolded Elise. "That's a dumb question."

"No, that's all right." Grandfather held up his hand and laughed. "I think I can probably answer that one. I suppose I have done something illegal at one time or the other. Only thing is, most of the things that are illegal these days are illegal because the Germans say so, not our own government. That's the only kind of illegal thing I've done."

"What did you do?" asked Elise. "Stay out after curfew? After nine?"

"Now wait a minute," he answered. "That's two questions already. I get a turn first."

"Oh, Grandfather," moaned Elise. "That's not fair."

"Sure it's fair. You asked me if I had ever done anything illegal, and I answered yes, at least illegal to the Germans. Now it's my turn, and my question is for Elise. I want to know if you're going to be a scientist, a concert pianist, or a linguist."

"Oh, that's easy," Elise shot back without hesitating. "None of those."

"So what are you going to be, then?" asked her grandfather.

Elise laughed. "That's two questions, but I'll tell you. I've decided I'm going to be an artist. I've already—"

She stopped in midsentence, as if she just realized she had said too much. Then she continued, a little more cautiously. "I've already been practicing some."

"Well, how come we haven't seen more of your drawings lately?" asked Grandfather. "The last things I remember seeing are the wonderful little sketches you used to hand out when you were younger."

Elise just grinned shyly. "I don't know," she said.

"I think she keeps a lot of them in a book," reported Peter. "It's kind of like a diary. I tried to look at it once, but as soon as I picked it up, she clobbered me and took it away."

"Oh, *that* kind of book," replied Grandfather. "I wonder what kinds of things she draws that they're so secret."

"They're not that secret." Elise fidgeted with her pole, looking uncomfortable. "They're pictures of the city mostly—buildings, people, horses, castles. It's just that I don't want everyone staring at them and saying things. I work on them in the afternoons, after we—"

Peter knew what his sister was about to say, and he was too afraid to look up.

"After we deliver papers," she finished.

"Really?" asked their grandfather. "What kind of papers are you two delivering?"

There was a silence, and Peter thought his grandfather was probably wondering what was wrong with such a simple question. He wanted her to say it, and he wanted her to be quiet at the same time.

"We're delivering Underground newspapers, Grandfather," Elise blurted out. Peter winced, waiting for an explosion of some sort, or at least for lightning to strike from the calm afternoon sky. But Grandfather Andersen didn't change his expression; he only settled back against the wooden piling and looked as if he were ready to hear a bedtime story. So Elise took a deep breath and continued.

"Three afternoons a week we get these newspapers—Underground newspapers—and we pack them into little bundles with old shirts and take them places." She was talking much faster than she usually did, kind of like a record player turned up to the next speed. "Peter gets a bundle and I get a bundle, and we used to take them to a dry cleaners, but somebody found out, and now we take them to a tailor shop."

Elise looked at her brother, as if she were waiting for him to fill in details. He still wasn't saying anything, just sat staring at his fishing pole, so she launched back into her story.

"The dry cleaner didn't get into trouble, though," Elise rattled on. "But there was this guy from school who followed us the first time we were supposed to deliver to the tailor, and he had a German officer with him. We hid behind an old lady in a butcher shop so they couldn't find us. Right, Peter?"

He mumbled something that sounded like "uh-huh," but Elise wasn't going to let Peter stay silent. "Say something," she ordered.

"Right," said Peter, checking his grandfather's expression. The old man still hadn't moved, so Peter cleared his throat. "But maybe it's not as bad as it sounds, Grandfather."

"Oh?" Grandfather Andersen arched his eyebrows. "How's that?"

"Well," continued Peter, finally warming up to the subject. "The guys at the newspaper are pretty nice, except for the one who writes a lot of the stories."

"Yeah," agreed Elise. "He's a grouch."

"But the man who prints it let me run the printing press, and he showed me a few things," added Peter. "And the guy—he's not so old, just a teenager—who gives us the newspapers is always making jokes. We call him Bent. He's pretty nice. We're even figuring out a way to get Uncle Morten out of prison."

Grandfather raised his eyebrows again at the mention of his younger son. "You know where Morten is?"

"Well, n-not exactly," Peter volunteered. "But I've been checking around. Listening to what the newspaper people say. I think he's either still at Vestre Prison in Copenhagen, or he's been moved to this new Shell House place. It's a Gestapo headquarters too."

"I see." Grandfather balanced his fishing pole on his knee. He had collected a few more wrinkles on his forehead. "It sounds as if you two are quite the experts. Now, how about the boy who was following you? Who was that?"

"Oh, him," groaned Peter. "That was Keld. He's in my class, and he's always on my case. Always has been."

"Keld . . . Poulsen?" asked Grandfather.

"Poulsen, yeah." Peter stopped pulling in his line. "How did you know?"

"You may not know about the Poulsen family, Peter, but his father is a Nazi."

Keld's dad a Nazi? What about Keld, then? That would explain a lot of things.

"You mean, his dad works for the Germans? I thought he didn't even have a dad." Peter couldn't remember how he had heard that—maybe someone at school had told him.

"His parents are divorced, and his father lives in Copenhagen," explained Grandfather. "The man used to work in the port office. When the Germans took over the country, he was one of the only ones who wanted to help them. Then all of a sudden this Poulsen fellow was gone, and I heard he had left the family to work at Gestapo headquarters in the big city."

Peter looked down through a crack in the thick boards at the inky dark green water underneath. It surged in with a swoosh, and then sucked back out. It made him a little queasy, so he looked back up.

"I didn't know that," said Elise for both of them. "Kind of makes me feel sorry for him. But he's still a bully."

Now Grandfather Andersen was scratching his chin, obviously thinking about something. He had set his pole aside.

"You're not going to tell Mom and Dad, are you?" asked Elise.

Grandfather looked from one face to the other and shook his head. He let out his breath and crossed his arms. "No, I'm not. But I believe *you* certainly are."

Peter looked down through the crack in the pier again. He could almost feel the air being blown up through the cracks ahead of a wave swell. "So will you go with us?" he asked hopefully. "Help us tell them?"

"Hmm, I might do that." Grandfather coughed again, then cleared his throat. "But before I do, you'd better tell me if there's anything else I should know."

The only sound for a couple of minutes was the steady swoosh of the waves under the pier. Peter was afraid to look up. Elise finally said something.

"Well, there was one other thing, Grandfather. We—I mean Peter found a note in Uncle Morten's Bible and . . ."

"Let me tell about that," interrupted Peter, looking up. "I found a note in Uncle Morten's Bible when we were over at his apartment with Dad. It had a name and address on it, and when we went there, it was some kind of Bible study. She was really nice, it turns out."

"Who was really nice?" asked Grandfather. "Lisbeth von Schreider?"

"How do you know all these people?" Peter couldn't imagine. First Keld Poulsen and his family, now Uncle Morten's girlfriend. Was there anyone Grandpa didn't know about?

Grandfather Andersen just chuckled. "Your uncle told me about her right after they met." Then he slowly got to his feet and clapped Peter on the back. "I'm his father, remember? We used to talk. She sounded like a nice girl, I think. So you met her? What did she say?"

"She was nice," replied Elise. "Really nice. I liked her. And everybody at her apartment talked as if she and Uncle Morten were still . . . you know . . . friends."

"Do you mean that she knows where he is?" asked Grandfather. "She's seen him?"

"No, no." Elise shook her head. "I don't think so. Nothing like that. One of the guys said they were praying for him all the time, for Uncle Morten to be released. I think that's all they knew, too."

"I see," replied Grandfather, looking disappointed. "That's good to hear anyway."

"Well," put in Peter, "I told them we were trying to figure out a way to get Uncle Morten out of prison too."

Grandfather only shook his head and looked over at his grandson with a sad, tired expression in his eyes.

"Peter," said Grandfather, "you know as well as I do that you're not going to do that." He cocked his head to look into Peter's eyes, his expression still kindly but firm. "Don't you?"

Peter could only nod. Deep inside, he thought he felt a little bubble of hope burst. No, he wasn't going to be able to rescue his uncle. *It was a dumb idea anyway,* he thought. And now, they were going to have to tell their parents everything about what they were doing with the newspaper. He breathed a sigh of relief, combed his hair with his fingers, and closed his eyes. Maybe it was better this way.

"Peter, grab it!" yelled Elise.

"What? Grab what?" Peter was still thinking about talking to his parents, but Elise had jumped to her feet and was running after her grandfather's fishing pole.

"Get it before it slips into the water!" shouted Elise once more. Peter was the closest to the pole, but it flashed by him before he caught on to what was happening. Elise made a desperate attempt to catch the pole, diving over Peter and grabbing it right on the edge of the pier.

"Got it!" Peter heard her say.

"Don't fall in," warned Grandfather, but by then Elise had rolled off Peter's lap and was sitting on the pier with the pole, pulling in the fish.

"You two were daydreaming," she grunted, "and here's the biggest fish in the ocean, pulling your pole into the Sound!"

"Here, let me help you," offered Peter.

"Too late," replied Elise. Her face was red, and she was sweating despite the cold. "I've got it now."

And she did have it, or at least something was splashing and struggling as Elise yanked it closer and tried to pull it free of the water. Just as it cleared the water, though, Peter heard a mighty snap, and Elise fell to her knees.

"The fishing pole!" she yelled. "It broke!"

Peter's first instinct was to grab Elise around the shoulders, trying to keep her from falling into the water. She stubbornly held on to her broken pieces of fishing pole, still reeling in her prize.

"I've still got it." She grimaced and yanked what was left of the pole. Peter wasn't sure how she held on, but he looked over the side with his grandfather to see if the fish was still there. With a mighty tug, Elise pulled an enormous flapping fish out of the water, and it shot straight up into Peter's face.

"Hey!" shouted Peter, falling backward with the fish. He

waved his arms wildly, but the fishing line only tangled up more. "Get this thing off me!"

While Grandfather laughed, Elise put down her broken pole and helped pull off the squirming fish as it flapped and puffed its gills in panic. It took a minute, but Peter finally crawled free of the tangle.

"I'll have to cut this apart," said Grandfather, pulling a small pocketknife from his pocket. "And look at the size of that rock-fish!"

"Must be as big as a dog." Peter crept closer, while the fish still gasped and puffed. It looked very much out of its element—alien, its eyes bulging like giant marbles. Peter measured the fish with his hands spread apart.

"Small dog," agreed Grandfather. "I've never seen one so close to shore. What do you think, Elise?"

Elise just grinned, looking especially pleased with herself. "Not bad," she said, examining her catch. She poked at it gently, then she looked back at the pile of tangled fishing line and broken pole. "But look at that poor pole."

"Don't worry about that." Grandfather Andersen dismissed the tangled mess with a wave of his hand. "It was worth it to see you pull that monster up here into Peter's lap." They all laughed once more at the thought.

"Attack of the killer rockfish." Elise cupped her hands in front of her face and snapped them like a fish mouth at her brother. He yelped and jumped away with a laugh.

Peter still wasn't sure what to make of the ugly creature. "Pretty good job, sis. Grandpa and I would have just watched the pole swim away if it wasn't for you. Even if you did pull that—that *thing* up in my face." He stuck out his hand, and she shook it.

"Well," declared Grandfather. "It's not herring, but it's quite good, especially the way your mother cooks it in a stew. It sure beats what little meat we've been able to get lately with our ration cards. Rockfish stew is pretty tasty."

"It's big all right," said Elise, poking gingerly at the fish. It puffed a few more times, eyes bulging. "They don't look as scary when they're in the fish market. Only thing is, now we need to get it home somehow."

Grandfather Andersen looked around and laughed once more. "Honestly, I hadn't thought of that. In fact, I didn't really think we were going to catch anything, much less a whale. Here, Peter, why don't you run back to the boathouse and find something you can bring your sister's trophy home in? I think there's a small stack of legal newspapers just inside the door."

There were, and Peter returned to the pier at a gallop with an armload of papers.

"Is this enough?" he asked.

"More than plenty," answered Grandfather. He took a handful of papers and quickly wrapped up the now dead fish. Then he turned back to Peter. "Here, take this home to your mother. Tell her I'll be over tonight to help you eat it." He handed the fish to Peter and put both his hands on Peter's shoulders. "I'll help you tonight, but you have to tell your mom and dad everything. No more secrets, understand?"

"We understand," Elise and Peter sang out at the same time. Tucking the huge fish under his arm, Peter dashed back up the pier. Elise followed along beside him, fishing poles over her shoulder. Two minutes later, they had stashed the poles in the boathouse and were on their way home.

"This is going to be a great dinner, I think," said Peter, feeling lighter than he had in months. "Even though Mom and Dad are probably going to go through the roof when they hear everything."

"I know they are," agreed Elise. "But maybe it's better this way."

By then Elise was looking the other way, up the street away from the harbor. Peter followed her glance and picked out the person she had noticed. Bent, from the newspaper. The teenager was riding his bicycle toward them, full speed.

"Hey, you two!" the boy shouted as soon as he was within earshot. Then he looked around to see if anyone else was close enough to hear them, and he lowered his voice to a whisper. "I thought I'd find you down here. We just found out from someone inside that the Nazis are going to raid our offices! Maybe in less than an hour."

Peter nearly dropped the fish. "So what do we do? We can't just leave the printing press there, can we?"

"It's already half taken apart," replied Bent, "but we need more help moving parts to the new place, and we have to do it without attracting attention. Come on!"

RAID

It was hard to run with the big fish under his arm, but Peter didn't know what else to do with it. He couldn't just put it down. Bent pedaled slowly while the twins jogged along beside him.

"What's in the package?" he asked, nodding curiously toward Peter. "It looks like a body."

"Kind of a body," Peter answered in between breaths. "Elise caught a whale, and we're going to have it for dinner."

"Hmm," said Bent. "Well, the Germans are going to catch themselves a printing press if we don't hurry up." With that he pulled ahead of the joggers, and they quickened their pace even more. They were almost to the dentist's office where the printing press was when he stopped.

"Okay, now look." Bent pulled over to the side and pretended to adjust something on the wheel. "We can't just go charging in and come out with big pieces of the printing press in our hands. It has to look normal. I have a backpack in the basement you can use. Fill it with stuff, and then carry it to the new building. Take different routes so you don't attract anybody's attention."

Peter and Elise nodded solemnly. *What if someone is watching?*

thought Peter, but he didn't dare ask. Bent was still leaning over his bike, not looking at them as he spoke almost in a whisper.

"Now go, but one at a time," the teenager told them. "I'll be right there."

Peter went first, followed soon after by Elise. He circled around the building, and after a quick look up and down the alley, he slipped into the basement.

Everything was torn apart. Kaspar was working feverishly on the press with a wrench, pulling off rollers and hoses, nuts and bolts. Everything was stacked in bags and boxes, carefully marked and numbered. He looked up, startled, when Peter walked in, but quickly returned to his work.

"Just you," he said. "Good. I need a few more hands to move this stuff." He set another roller down on the table next to him, picked up a pen, and marked something on a bag.

"Where are we taking it?" asked Peter. He set the fish down by a small pile of springs on a table next to the door. The man didn't seem to hear Peter's question, but by then Bent and Elise had made it down to the basement.

"Hey, Bent, where are we taking this stuff?" Peter asked again.

"Another basement just down the street," replied the older boy. "Domus Department Store. Actually, it's not part of the store, but there's this basement that they've used for storing things. I'll show you."

As he talked, Bent fitted Elise with a backpack and gave Peter a large paper shopping bag with string handles and "Domus— Best Buys for Less" printed on the side. Then he started stuffing rollers and other parts into the two bags from the piles the old man had already made. He had his own large shopping bag as well.

"Follow me now," said Bent, carefully dropping one last gear in his bag. Peter wondered how they were going to put it all back together again, but he didn't say anything. He just hoped they didn't run into any curious German soldiers on this shopping trip.

The three separated themselves by about ten paces as they walked down the street. Several larger stores attracted Saturday shoppers; this was one of the busier commercial streets in the city. At the end of the block, Bent circled around the large department store, ignoring the crowds going in and out. Instead, he went around to the back and found the loading dock. He looked both ways before stepping up; then he pushed his way through a large swinging door. Peter and Elise did the same.

Inside, it took Peter's eyes a moment to get used to the dim, dingy loading dock area. Boxes were stacked all over, and at first they couldn't see where Bent had disappeared to. Then he waved at them from one of three doors that led off to the side. Peter shifted the heavy bag to his other hand and followed Bent and Elise through the door and down a small flight of stairs. *This is really a dungeon,* he thought. *All it needs are torches on the walls.*

Torches would have helped, Peter decided. He paused for a moment, took a deep breath, and tried to command the hair on the back of his neck to settle down.

"Down here," came Bent's voice, and Peter thought he could just make out Elise turning to the right through another doorway. Once he followed her into the basement room a light flipped on.

"There," said Bent, setting his load down in the middle of a dusty floor. "Perfect place for an Underground newspaper." He smiled and stood with his arms crossed in a small pool of light under a bulb dangling on a short wire. "Underground."

Peter set his load down next to Elise's and tried to imagine what might be crouching in the shadowy corners of that room. It looked big enough, though a lot of it was taken up with dusty old piles—broken display cases, clothes racks, that sort of thing.

"You're really going to run the newspaper down here?" asked Elise, hugging her elbows. "It's kind of creepy."

"Maybe," replied Bent. "But it's fine for now, at least until they catch up with us again." Then he headed for the door. "Come on, we have to hurry. There's not much time left."

By the fourth trip down the stairs, Peter started to find his way a little better, and the shadows didn't seem quite as creepy once his eyes got used to the blackness. He stood with Elise in the middle of the room, next to a large pile of parts that was the disassembled press.

"Maybe you're right, Bent," Peter told the teenager, who was just coming in the door. "This is kind of a neat place for the newspaper. It's quiet."

Everyone paused for a moment to see if they could hear anything. The only sound was a trickle through one of the black, rusty pipes that laced the ceiling, and a shuffling coming down the stairs.

"Just us," called the reporter. He was carrying the last load—his typewriter and some files. The old printer was right behind him with an armload of tools.

"You didn't see anyone?" asked Bent.

"Nobody," answered the reporter. "We're out of there. Now comes the fun part of putting this thing back together again. You'd think that after doing this three or four times it would get easier. Thank goodness our friend warned us in time."

"Our friend?" asked Elise. Peter didn't know what the man was talking about either. The printer didn't answer right away, just cleared his throat.

"Um, never mind, kids," he said, looking embarrassed. "You don't need to know. Just a friend."

"Yeah, thanks for your help," put in Bent. "We'll take care of it from here."

But now Peter wasn't quite ready to leave. "We can help you set it back up," he volunteered, "if you just show us how."

"No, Christian, we better get going," said Elise, heading for the door. "Mom will start to wonder, and—" She slapped her forehead and groaned. "You know what we forgot? My fish!"

"The fish?" asked Peter. "What happened to it?"

But Elise was already out and up the stairs, taking them two at a time. Peter ran out after her.

"See you guys Monday, okay?" he called out behind him.

"*If* we can get this thing back and running," replied the printer.

Peter sprinted to catch up with his sister; she was already way down the alley when he emerged from the dark stairway. He stood still just for a moment to get his eyes used to the light again, then took off after her.

"Hey," he panted a minute later. "Wait up! What's the hurry anyway?"

"I want to get the fish out before anybody gets there."

"Anybody" of course meant the Germans, and now Peter knew why his sister was hurrying so. By the time he caught up with her, they were at the entrance to the old newspaper office. They both skidded to a stop, and Peter looked around.

"I don't see anybody," he panted. "And you sure run fast these days."

Elise just slipped inside, and Peter followed. Everything was cleared out except for a couple of old chairs in the corner and a pile of something wrapped in newspaper. The prize fish!

"There it is," said Peter, stepping over to retrieve the package. He picked it up, tossed it once in his hands, and then flipped it over to Elise.

"Hey!" she told him. "Watch it!"

"Good catch, Elise." Peter grinned. "But your fish is starting to smell a little."

"It is not," she said defensively. "It's only been about an hour. We'll just take it home right away."

"Fine with me," answered Peter. He was about to turn and head for the door when something bright caught his eye. He looked down at the table where the fish had been. More printing press parts!

"Hey, Elise, wait a minute." He motioned his sister back. "Look what was here behind your fish."

"Oh no," groaned Elise. "It looks like some more pieces to that printing press. We better run back over with them."

Peter quickly scooped up the pile of springs and knobs and

stuffed them into his coat pocket.

"Fine," he said with an edge to his voice. "Let's just get out of here, okay? I don't want to meet any Germans today."

Peter carefully looked up and down the alley before they went out the back door, then once again made their way toward the new basement hiding place. But they hadn't taken more than ten steps out the door when a booming voice from behind stopped them in their tracks.

"You two!" shouted a man with a thick German accent. "Stop right there!"

"Should we run?" Peter whispered to Elise, grabbing her elbow. Once they were out on the street, they would be able to duck into a store or hide in a crowd. But before they could decide, a group of soldiers appeared ahead of them.

"I said stop right there!" boomed the voice, and this time Peter and Elise slowly turned to see a German officer striding quickly down the alley toward them.

"Look innocent," Elise whispered out of the side of her mouth. "And get rid of those printing press parts!"

The Germans were still a few doors down. Maybe they wouldn't notice. Peter reached into his coat pocket for a handful of parts and looked for somewhere to hide them. Next to him, Elise's ugly fish head was sticking out from the newspaper they had wrapped their catch in. Maybe it would work.

With a very small movement that he hoped would not catch anyone's attention, Peter leaned over and stuffed his handful of springs and parts into the gaping mouth of the fish. As the Germans came charging down the alley, he hid another handful, then another. Somehow he stuffed everything that was in his pocket into the belly of the big fish. Elise didn't even look down, though Peter knew she could see what he was doing out of the corner of her eye.

"What are you children doing here?" barked the officer as soon as he reached the twins. Without looking in his face, Peter knew who it was. The man with the crooked nose. The one who had been with Keld the other day. The major. The officer motioned for the other soldiers to check the back door of the dentist's office. "You were just in there, no?"

Elise quickly held up her fish. "We were just going home after fishing. See?"

The major only wrinkled his nose and looked over at the office. Five soldiers, rifles drawn, came charging through from the front.

"Nothing in there except a dentist's office," said the last one out, a tall, lanky-looking sergeant. "The same person must have tipped them off again."

The major, fire in his eyes, whirled on the twins once more.

"You didn't answer my question," he barked. "What were you doing in there?"

Afraid to look in the man's eyes, Peter looked at the alley. It was a little muddy, with slush patches here and there. The major marched around to stand in front of him, and Peter could see the man's shiny boots. Peter looked up straight into the man's shining silver jacket buttons.

"Just, j-just on . . . on our way home," Peter sputtered. "Fishing. Fish."

"That is certainly the ugliest fish I have seen in a long time," pronounced the major. He bent down lower to examine Elise's fish. "Unwrap it."

With Peter's help, Elise nervously peeled back the paper. The officer bent down once more, looking like a customer in a fish market.

"Hmm, yes, that will do, I think. I've been unable to find a suitable fish for the general's dinner tomorrow." He was grinning now—an evil Big Bad Wolf kind of grin that only made Peter sweat more. Then he turned to one of the soldiers standing next to him. "Schmidt, take this fish with you. Have the cook at headquarters prepare it in the stew for the general tomorrow."

"Yes, sir, Major Mueller." The soldier stepped forward and took the enormous fish from Elise and Peter. Peter could only close his eyes and imagine what would happen to them when the cook found what was inside the fish. The major turned to them once more.

"Now, are you two going to explain what you were doing here at this time?" asked the German, rocking back on his heels. "Having your teeth cleaned perhaps?" He almost spit at Peter as he bent down to look into Peter's eyes.

Again Peter was tongue-tied, and he struggled to say something that made sense. He looked over at Elise, but her look made him turn quickly away. Both of them knew the dentist's office was closed for the day. Peter couldn't think of a good story.

"W-we were just fishing," Peter mumbled. "Just going home."

"Just helping to move the printing press, you say?" mocked the officer. "Just took a few parts of a printing press—thought you'd take them home for fun, did you? Maybe do a little printing in the living room?"

Peter shrugged. Even though he was sweating, he felt as cold as ice. As much as he tried, he couldn't stop shivering.

"Oh, I'm so sorry you're cold," said Major Mueller, stooping down again to meet Peter's and Elise's eyes. He put his hands on their shoulders and pushed them together. Peter wanted to pull away, but soldiers were now standing in a ring around them. A truck pulled up behind them, but no one moved.

"Now listen here, you two." The major looked first at Elise, then over at Peter. His hand felt like an eagle claw on Peter's shoulder, and he winced in pain. "You can't squirm out of this one with your little stories of going home. Little innocent children who don't know what's going on, are you? Well, we will see about that. Whatever you're doing with this printing press, it's illegal and stupid." He raised his voice again and shook Peter by the shoulders. Elise began to cry.

"Do you know what your parents are going to do to you when they find out? Do you?" shouted the major. "Do you?"

Peter didn't know, but he thought he wouldn't mind finding out at this point. Anything to get out of this alley, away from this man. Major Mueller took a deep breath and lowered his voice.

"See here. I'm going to make you a deal," he said, "and I'm only going to say it once."

Peter closed his eyes. *This can't be happening to us,* he thought. *We're not really here.* He could hear Elise sniffling, and the major kept talking in his nasal, accented speech.

"Are you listening?" demanded the man. Peter and Elise both nodded. Now Peter felt like crying.

"I said I'm only going to offer you this deal once, and once only," Major Mueller went on. Then his voice softened for a moment. "You take me to where the printing press is. Just tell us where they took it. Then you take your fish back, go home, and forget this ever happened, *ja*?" He laughed, a loud, nervous laugh. The man's breath, so close, made Peter want to pull back even more. "We forget it ever happened, and your mama will never know! No one gets hurt, *ja*?"

Peter stiffened at the thought of telling where the printing press was. Bent, Kaspar, and the others were probably all still there, piecing it back together. They might even be looking for the missing parts, the ones hiding in the fish stomach. They would have to do without them for sure now. Peter hoped the pieces weren't too important.

"How about it, kids?" asked Major Mueller once more. He straightened up, crossed his arms, and glanced over at the idling truck. Then he blew on his hands to warm them up. "I'm getting cold and very impatient. Let's not make it unpleasant. Where is the printing press?" He stomped his foot for effect.

A minute went by, and one of the soldiers cleared his throat. All the while, the major's expression grew darker and darker, like an approaching thunderstorm. And still Peter and Elise could say nothing. They stood there, silent, another minute, then two, and then the major blew up.

"Stupid kids!" he hissed in German. "Stupid, stupid children. We *will* find out what we need to know, but it will not be so pleasant now." Then he turned to his sergeant, issued a spattering of commands, and turned back to Peter and Elise with a sweep of his hand.

"Get them in the truck!" he commanded. "I'm tired of standing out here in the stupid slush, in this stupid alley, with these stupid children!" He scraped the mud from his boots with a piece of broken glass and flicked it at Peter before he turned away. It hit Peter on the leg. For a moment, the German stood still, as if trying to make up his mind about something. Then he glanced back over his shoulder and looked straight at Elise. She looked down, and Peter could see that her eyes were red and swollen.

"If you children believe you can make a fool of me," warned Major Mueller, "you are sadly mistaken." Then he climbed up into the cab of the truck and slammed the door behind him.

From behind, soldiers grabbed Peter and Elise, hauling them up into the back of the canvas-covered truck. Others, guns drawn, climbed up after them; Peter and Elise were sandwiched between two burly soldiers in gray-green uniforms. Peter couldn't see the soldier who had taken their fish.

One of the soldiers with them knocked twice on the window of the truck cab, where Major Mueller was sitting, and the truck lurched away down the alley. Exhaust fumes filled the back of the truck, one of the soldiers lit a cigarette, and Peter thought he was going to be sick.

We should have left the fish to rot, he thought.

HEART OF THE ENEMY CAMP

"Where are you taking us?" Peter asked after they had traveled only a few minutes. The wooden bench they were sitting on was hard and unforgiving, and Peter had to hold on to Elise's leg as they rounded a corner. The soldier next to him just shrugged and blew smoke in their faces while the others laughed.

"You'll find out," said the young German. "Not far."

The soldiers all took turns pointing their rifles out the back of the truck and making shooting sounds. One of them would pretend to shoot into the street, then say something in German, and the rest would respond with a chorus of laughter. Peter closed his eyes, fighting back the tears and the overwhelming fear.

At least the German was right; only five minutes later, the truck stopped to let the major out, then pulled on a little farther to let everyone else pile out the back. They were in a courtyard driveway of a large three-story brick building that Peter didn't recognize, at least not from the back. The soldiers pulled their rifles out again and shoved Peter and Elise to a doorway, a service entrance.

"Do you know where we are?" Peter asked his sister as they were hustled inside.

She looked over at him, the fear still showing in her eyes, and tripped over a step. Peter reached down and helped her up while a soldier growled behind them.

"Come on!" said the soldier, the same one who had blown smoke in their faces.

"I think we're still downtown somewhere," whispered Elise as they climbed the stairs. Peter held tightly to his sister's hand. "Looks like one of those big office buildings."

"Don't talk," ordered the soldier, while another one opened the door at the top of the long stairwell. The building had once been quite fancy, Peter thought, but it was looking a little sad around the edges now. He heard more trucks and army cars coming and going down in the courtyard.

The top of the stairway opened up into a large room filled with desks, telephones, typewriters, and file cabinets. It smelled of stale smoke and looked like a typical office, except that half of the people working there—men and women—were wearing gray German army uniforms. A couple of telephones rang. The only other sound Peter could hear was the constant clatter of typewriters. Major Mueller was standing next to one of the desks at the other side of the room, and motioned impatiently with his hand for the soldiers to bring Peter and Elise to him.

The woman at the desk looked up briefly as the twins came close, and for a moment, Peter couldn't believe his eyes. There was only a slight hesitation before the woman looked back down and continued her typing. Peter tugged at Elise's hand, and she squeezed back. She had seen too.

He wanted to be wrong, but there was no mistaking: It was Lisbeth von Schreider!

"Come, come," said Major Mueller, who was pacing. "We will not wait any longer." Then he pointed to a small room. "Put them in there."

"In there" turned out to be another small office, not much bigger than a closet. It was stripped of its furniture, though it did have a tiny window. The window didn't open, but if Peter stood on his tiptoes, he could make out a little of the street below.

"I know where we are now," he told Elise after the door had been shut on them and they were alone. "North side of town. I can see Esrum Boulevard down there."

But Elise wasn't looking out any windows. She slid to the floor with her face in her hands.

"Elise, are you all right?" asked Peter.

She didn't answer, just sobbed. Peter sat down next to her and put his hand on her shoulder. He wished he could cry just then too. But after everything that had happened that afternoon, and especially after seeing Lisbeth von Schreider, he felt as if he were in shock.

Lisbeth, working for the Germans! And we thought she was so nice! Peter slammed his fist against the floor. *What a traitor! We told her everything about wanting to get Uncle Morten out of prison. Good thing we didn't say anything about* The Free Dane *to her. Or did we?*

Elise just kept crying, and Peter patted her back. When he couldn't think of anything else to be mad about, the tears slowly came to his eyes, and he sat there with his sister, not saying anything.

After a few minutes, Peter wiped his eyes and stood up. "We'll get out of here, Elise," he told her, trying to sound braver than he felt. "Dad will come and get us, or something."

"But Dad doesn't even know where we are," said Elise. "Grandpa is probably just showing up at home, and they're wondering where we are with the fish."

"Well, if you think we're in trouble now," said Peter, trying to make his sister smile, "wait until the general bites into his fish. Ow!" He held his mouth, pretending to be in pain. Elise smiled, but only weakly. Then Peter went back to looking out the small window, watching the few people down on the street.

"I'm not sure how you can make jokes right now, Peter," she

said, dabbing at her eyes with the corner of her blouse. "What are we going to do?"

"I don't know." Peter pulled his hair and stared out the window. "We could yell out the window."

"It doesn't open."

"Maybe we could break it and escape."

"Peter, not even your little shoulders could fit through."

Peter examined their tiny window once more, but he knew his sister was right. It was really only a small picture frame for light; he could barely see through it down to the street where people were walking.

"Yeah, I know," he sighed. "And even if we could get through it—"

"You know we can't do that, Peter."

"That's what I mean, Elise. But the roof out there is just about straight up and down. We could jump down to the street—"

"Two stories down to the concrete?"

"Yeah, right," concluded Peter, pacing in front of the window. "Well, if only we could—"

"Could what?" asked Elise. "What can anyone do? The soldiers would just grab anybody who tried to help us, the way they grabbed us, and throw them into a prison, or do whatever they want."

"Elise, don't be so, so—" Peter shook his head. He didn't like it when his sister seemed to give up like this.

"Don't be so what?"

"I don't know." Peter kept his eyes on the street. "I just have this feeling that we're going to get out of this. I just do."

Looking down on the street, Peter could tell that there weren't as many people out now. A few rode by on bicycles, but most people were probably home—where Peter wished he was. After half an hour of watching, he suddenly noticed two figures at the end of the street. They were different from the rest: two men, one taller than the other, going from door to door, as if they were searching for the right number. As they got a little closer, Peter was sure. He turned back to Elise.

"What did I tell you," he announced. "You'll never guess who's coming down the street to rescue us!"

"Peter," said Elise from her spot on the floor, "I'm not in the mood for one of your jokes."

"I'm not kidding! Take a look!"

Elise wiped her eyes with the sleeve of her blouse and slowly got to her feet. She looked as if she didn't believe her brother for a minute. Still, she peeked out the window in the direction Peter was pointing, and her eyes lit up too.

"How did Dad and Grandpa—" she started to ask. "How did they know where to come? I don't get it."

The twins had no time to figure it out, however, because a guard came to their door just then, rattling a key.

"This way," grunted the young German. He motioned with his head for them to move out of the little room. Then he took their arms and guided them down a hallway and around a corner into another small room. This time, however, there were a couple of chairs and a round table, so Peter and Elise sat down. Both of them heaved a sigh.

"I hope Dad gets us out of here quick," whispered Peter. Elise nodded in agreement. Their father would probably be coming up the front steps of the building they were in just about now.

They didn't have to sit long. Their next visitor was Major Mueller, who came to the door in a flurry of key rattling and heel clicking. The guard stood at attention as the major entered.

Peter couldn't look at the man's face, not after the way he had yelled at them back in the alley. Besides, Major Mueller's crooked nose was downright unpleasant to look at. Maybe the officer should have been wearing boxing trunks, rather than a stiff gray uniform with an evil-looking eagle over his left chest pocket. Everything was in place, from the red and blue medals glittering on his chest to the buttoned shoulder pads. And everything was shiny—especially his tall black boots. At the same time, everything about him seemed to have a kind of dark glow. Peter shiv-

ered when the major stepped over to the table, almost as if a cold
breeze followed him in. No one said a word.

"Well?" demanded Major Mueller, rocking up and down on
his heels and toes as he had back in the alley. There was a moment
of silence, and Peter studied the reflection of the dim light in the
major's boots. Then the officer slammed something down on the
table, and Peter and Elise both looked up, startled. There sat a
copy of *The Free Dane*, a pad of lined paper, and two sharpened
pencils. Peter caught a glimpse of the major's eyes, and he saw
fire.

"I have no further patience for baby-sitting." The man spat out
each word as if it stung his lips. "None." He stroked his chin and
set his jaw. "You will tell us all about this—this propaganda
sheet—and you will tell us everything you know. Names. De-
scriptions of the criminals involved. Tell me directly or write it
down on these pads. How many. Their contacts. Your contacts.
Distribution. Everything!" He reached out his hand as if he would
choke Peter on the spot. "Everything! Now!"

Peter and Elise looked at their feet, both terrified. But there
was an unspoken agreement. Neither would say a word, unless . . . Peter shook his head. He couldn't think that far ahead.
The major kept up his shouting, then grabbed Peter by the front
of the shirt and shook him.

"Are you listening?" he asked. Peter nodded yes, terrified.
"Then look at me. How old are you?"

"Twelve." Peter would give him that. "And my father is coming to get me."

"Only twelve, are you?" Another evil smile curled the major's
lips, and his voice softened again to the sickening honey tone he
had used on them earlier. "Only twelve? The Resistance is getting
desperate, using such children." Then he released his clawlike
hold. "But it's sick. You should be home, eating dinner. And so
should I, for that matter, but not in this insane little country."

As much as he hated to admit it, Peter had to agree with him
there. Still, he didn't say a word. There was a knock on the door,

and the major snapped around to challenge the unlucky person who was interrupting.

"What is it?" he demanded. A young soldier entered, then stepped over to whisper something in the major's ear. A slight grin flickered across Major Mueller's face, and he nodded.

"Fine," he told the soldier. "Don't tell them a thing yet. Not until I give the word."

The soldier clicked his heels and was gone. The major closed the door once more and turned to Peter and Elise.

"Well, I must admit I'm surprised how quickly your father found us," said Major Mueller. He wrinkled his brow, as if trying to figure a math problem. "Now, how would he have come here so quickly, I wonder? Well, regardless, your father and grandfather are here right now, pounding on our door downstairs."

Major Mueller stared directly at the twins, but both Peter and Elise kept blank expressions. "They say they saw you being taken away, and they want to take you home. You'd like that, wouldn't you? Wouldn't you, Lars and Evy?" He grinned broadly and crossed his arms in front of him, waiting for a reaction. "You see, we already know more about you than you think. Lars and Evy Petersen. Your father told us all about you."

Despite his fright, Peter had to smile inside. *Dad told them all about us, all right. Including the wrong names!*

"How did you find out all that?" Peter acted surprised, trying to find a way to play the major's game.

"Never mind," replied Major Mueller. "We told them you weren't here, but that we would check around. It's up to you now to make a choice. Tell us what we need to know and leave with Papa, or stay here for a more unpleasant time. As our guests, of course, and as an example to others. So, what will it be? Would you like to return in a few minutes with your father?"

Peter felt sure that he and Elise were thinking the same thing. *We can't tell*, he thought. *We just can't tell and get those other guys in trouble. There's no telling what might happen to them if they were put in prison.*

"I'm very sorry, sir." Elise was doing her best now to look brave, even though her eyes were puffy from crying. "We can't tell you anything we don't know. We were just trying to get home with our fish."

Peter remembered what his Uncle Morten had told him once about telling the truth to the enemy. It reminded him again about the Bible story when Rahab hid the Hebrew spies at Jericho, and then lied about where they were hiding. *I guess this is another Rahab situation,* he thought. *We're not going to be telling the truth to these enemies. Not now, not ever.*

"I see," replied the major. "Once more, the fish story." He picked up the newspaper, an issue of *The Free Dane* that Peter remembered quite clearly delivering a couple of weeks earlier. On the cover was a great little sketch of a Danish country church by the mystery artist.

"We hear about these filthy little papers," said the major, waving *The Free Dane* in the air. "And it makes my stomach turn. Lies, all of it! And where do think you get all these lies? You either make them up on the spot, or they're fed to you by the idiot British! Then you go printing these rags up in every basement in Denmark, and you think you're some kind of heroes."

He slammed the paper down on the table, and Peter looked away.

"Do you know how much you're hurting your country, as well as the German Reich, by helping these kinds of criminals?"

Peter squirmed in his seat but didn't say a word. Maybe the man would finish his speech and give up. Someone rapped on the door once more, and the major rolled his eyes in disgust.

"What is it now?" he fumed.

"Excuse me, sir," came a muffled young woman's voice from the other side of the door. Peter was pretty sure it wasn't Lisbeth. "I'm sorry to bother you, but I just have two quick questions. Those two men looking for their kids are still out in the front office, and they won't go away, no matter what we tell them. What do you want me to do? And then also, there's a truck going down to Gestapo headquarters in Copenhagen in a few minutes. Do you need anything while it's down there?"

The major took a deep, impatient breath, and then cracked the door a few inches to talk with his secretary. "Number one, I don't care what you tell those men. Tell them their kids were taken to the other side of town and released. Push them out the door—do whatever you need to do. And number two, no, I don't need anything in Copenhagen right now. Maybe a bottle of—" He looked back at the kids, and his face lit up with a dark idea.

"No, wait a minute, Fraulein Zeiler," he said. "I just thought of something." He chuckled and clapped his hands together. "Yes, this is perfect. Tell the rescuers out front that we have no idea where their two children are, and express my sincere sympathies to them. We will, however, keep a special watch out for them.

"Then have a guard accompany these two on the truck to the city. We will have them placed in the Shell House prison for a time—until their memories improve. I will phone ahead to explain the entire situation there to the officer in charge." Then he looked at Peter and Elise with a stare so icy and evil that it made Peter shiver. "This will be a unique learning experience for them."

The major brushed off his uniform and slipped out the door without another word. As the door slammed behind him, Peter could hear him muttering more instructions to the woman.

"I don't have time for this baby-sitting nonsense. We'll just let Copenhagen play with them for a time. A few bruises here and there, and they'll find their tongues right away. I have a dinner engagement tonight, or I would personally tend to this matter." The man laughed again, and his voice faded down the hall.

They were alone once again, and Peter tried not to start crying. Instead, he crossed his arms and shook. Elise was slumped over in the corner.

"Dear Father," Peter heard his sister praying, quietly whispering. He wanted to pray along with her, so he closed his eyes and listened to his sister continue. "We can't, we just can't handle this. It's too scary," she prayed. "Please, please, get us out of this.

Help us find our family again. Help them not to give up on us, or worry too much. In Jesus' name."

"Amen," Peter finished Elise's prayer, and he meant it. He opened his eyes and somehow managed to smile at his sister.

WELCOME TO THE SHELL HOUSE

Any other time a trip to Copenhagen would have been exciting for the twins. This time, though, it was all Peter and Elise could do just to hold on to the stiff wooden benches in the back of the army truck. Peter wished for a pillow to sit on, a blanket—anything to cushion the bumps. This was not a friendly way to travel.

Maybe that's why German soldiers are so grouchy all the time, he thought, *because they have to ride around in the back of these horrible trucks.*

He couldn't see them in the gloom, but Peter gagged from the smoke of the two soldiers, who seemed to have an endless supply of cigarettes between them. The exhaust from the back of the truck, sucked up into the place where they were sitting, wasn't much better. Every once in a while, the soldiers' faces would light up in the flare of a match. One of those times, Peter caught a quick glance of Elise, sandwiched between the soldiers on the bench. She was holding on to the bench with white knuckles, eyes closed, looking more weak and ragged than Peter had ever seen her before.

"How's it going, Elise?" Peter called when the truck idled at a corner somewhere.

"First class," replied Elise. Peter had to smile at his sister's courage. *Maybe we'll make it out of this fix after all*, he thought. He had felt a little better since they had prayed. He was just as scared but a little more ... a little more what? He wasn't quite sure. A little more protected, he finally decided.

Suddenly the truck lurched to a stop again, and the engine shut down. It seemed they had been in the back of that awful truck all night, though it was probably more like an hour.

"Out! Hurry UP!" yelled a shrill voice from outside, even before the canvas back flap had been pulled away. The soldiers who had been sitting with them jumped to their feet and poked Peter and Elise with the stubs of their rifles. One caught Peter right under the ribs.

"Ow!" he yelled. The jab brought tears to Peter's eyes, but he got up and shuffled to the back of the truck. He was collecting a full set of bruises. Someone finally pulled back the canvas, but it was almost as dark outside as it had been inside the back of the truck. A bright flashlight shined in their faces.

"Welcome to the Shell House and beautiful Copenhagen," announced a sarcastic voice behind the flashlight. *The Shell House!* Peter's mind flashed back to the conversation he had overheard at the newspaper office, when the two men had talked about the British bombing this place. But he didn't have time to think about that right now.

Peter shaded his eyes from the light and tried to make out who was talking. It looked like a tall German officer. Then he felt the end of a rifle nudge him in the back, and Peter and Elise climbed down out of the truck. They stood in the light of the flashlight, shivering.

"I understand you're visiting us for a short while to discuss a few things about the newspaper business," said the voice. "We'll be very happy to hear what you have to say, to ensure your visit will be a brief one." Then the light flashed straight into Peter's face. "I don't believe we've ever had guests as young as you, but we will do our best to see that you are quite . . . er . . . comfortable. Follow me."

The light snapped around, and Peter could make out the shape of a German officer's high-peaked cap. He and Elise stumbled behind the cap, rifles in their backs, across a small driveway, and then into the large office building.

Once inside, Peter could see that the man behind the flashlight was short and stocky, almost fat. His hat seemed to teeter on the top of a bald head, and every once in a while, the man would glance back to see that they were keeping up. His face reminded Peter of a prune.

"The boy in here"—Officer Prune waved at a door—"and the girl over there." He waved across the hall.

"Couldn't we—" Peter started to ask as he was shoved from behind through the doorway, but the door slammed shut before he could finish. He stumbled into the darkness, not knowing if he was in a large or a small room. He stood there, peering into the dark, and then he crouched down.

"Couldn't we at least be in the same room?" Peter whispered.

He still was unable to see a thing when he heard someone coming down the hall. The footsteps stopped, then a key turned in the door's lock. A moment later, light flooded the room. A man stepped in and stood staring at Peter. He was in his mid-forties, stocky and bald, and he wore a rumpled white shirt with the sleeves rolled up and gray slacks—no uniform. Then he smiled, almost in the same way as Major Mueller.

"Well, you and your sister seem to have gotten yourselves into some major trouble, haven't you?" The man came over to Peter, helped him to his feet, and walked him over to a table with two chairs. Peter didn't want the man to touch him, but he was too scared to pull away. The rest of the room—about the size of the Andersen family's living room—was bare, except for the light bulb that hung in the center.

"Please, sit down and let's talk," said the man. He actually sounded concerned. But the way he talked reminded Peter of someone. Peter still didn't say anything, only sat stiffly in his chair, staring straight ahead.

"I understand you're from Helsingor," said the man, looking casually at his fingernails. "Me too. In fact, that's why they sent me in to talk with you tonight, because they thought we might know some of the same people—kind of speak the same language, you know? My son goes to school there. You might know him—Keld Poulsen?"

Peter stiffened even more and tried to keep his eyes from bulging. *Keld's father!*

"You know him?" asked Mr. Poulsen.

"I've heard the name," croaked Peter.

"Terrific!" said the man, leaning his chair back and crossing his arms. "Then you probably go to the same school. You live in the Star Street area?"

"Axeltorv Street," replied Peter. He bit his tongue, not meaning to give the man any information. But Mr. Poulsen was not at all like his son. This man was actually friendly. And after everything Peter had been through that day, it felt good to talk to someone who wasn't yelling at him.

"Listen," said Mr. Poulsen. "I really want to apologize for what you and your sister have been through tonight. They told me just a little bit. Between you and me, I can't understand what they're thinking. I mean, how old are you? Thirteen? Like my youngest boy, Keld?"

"Twelve," replied Peter, not looking up.

"Well," continued Mr. Poulsen, "it makes me a little angry to think of dragging a pair of fine kids like you and your sister all the way down here to Copenhagen. I think someone wants to make an example of you, make it known that the Nazis are tough and that they won't let anyone get away with things. Even kids. Maybe *especially* kids. I want to help you out. Understand what I'm saying?"

Peter wondered for a moment if he should answer, then gave

in. "I understand," he told Mr. Poulsen. He eased up a little in his chair. *Maybe this guy is different,* thought Peter. *At least, he sounds like he understands kids.*

"Well, I would be scared too if I were you and I'd gotten myself into this kind of fix." Then he looked around, as if someone else might be in the room with them, and lowered his voice. "Listen," he whispered. "Can you keep your voice down? I'm not sure, but I think they have microphones planted in this room. Talk real low, you know, and we can have more of a private conversation."

"Really?" said Peter in his regular voice. Then he caught himself and whispered, "Really?"

"Yeah." Mr. Poulsen leaned over the table and whispered again. "Now listen. I really want to help you and your sis, but you have to give me a hand. I have to go back to the guys in the uniforms, like old pruneface there, and be able to convince them to let you go back home. They're pretty stern, but I know how to tell them what they want to hear. You want to go back home, don't you?"

"Sure," Peter whispered back. He decided Mr. Poulsen wasn't like his son at all. At least, he didn't act like him.

"Good boy. Now, tell me what was happening there in that alley. You know, I used to go to that dentist . . . what's his name?"

"Dr. Talbro."

"Right, Dr. Talbro. Sounds like an incredible place for an Underground newspaper, don't you think?"

What if I say yes? thought Peter. *Does that mean I'm saying I knew about the Underground newspaper?* He bit his tongue, then just shrugged. "I suppose it could be, if someone wanted to," Peter finally mumbled.

Mr. Poulsen's expression only changed for a half-second, but Peter thought he saw a flash of darkness, just like in Major Mueller's eyes. Then the man smiled again.

"Okay now, son, take me through the alley. I'm on your side, remember? But I can't help you get away from these guys—these,

these goons—if you don't at least help me understand what was going on. I promise you won't be hurt, as long as I can help it." He took a breath. "Now, you and your sister were helping the newspaper move, right? And everyone left you behind?"

"Who?" Peter could hardly focus his eyes anymore, and his mind felt as sharp as a bowl of day-old oatmeal. Still, he couldn't just come out and tell this man about their friends at the newspaper. He just couldn't.

"The people with the printing press, remember?" The man's voice grew louder, a little more impatient. He seemed to forget about the whispering and the microphones. "Don't you remember seeing people coming in and out of the dentist's office?"

"Oh, those people," Peter finally said, after thinking for a moment. "Yeah, I remember seeing people coming out."

"Now we're getting somewhere!" Mr. Poulsen rubbed his hands together. "Who did you see? Did you recognize them?"

Peter rubbed his chin and thought for a moment. "I recognized one person. Mrs. Engelmann from down the street. She's ninety, I think. Somebody said she was having a new set of teeth put in. Oh, but that must have been Friday. The office is closed on Saturday."

Mr. Poulsen's eyes flashed dark again, and he slammed his palm against the table. "Listen, kid, I'm not playing games with you." Then he caught himself and switched back to his soft tone. "Okay, I'm sorry. This is hard for me too, you know. I don't want to see you or your sister get hurt. If you don't tell me what you know, somebody else is going to come in here, and they're not going to be as nice as me. Now, let's start from the beginning. Once more. Tell me what you were doing with the newspaper. We need to know where they moved."

The questions lasted more than an hour while Peter tried to think of new ways to say nothing at all. But after going around in circles with his questions, Mr. Poulsen slowly gave up all appearances of being Mr. Nice Guy, and got more and more irritated as the night wore on. The man stood up, paced around, smoked, even pounded the wall a couple of times for effect. But even Mr. Poulsen's theatrics couldn't keep Peter's eyelids from getting heavier and heavier, and his mind from getting foggier and foggier.

"Can't I lie down somewhere and go to sleep?" Peter asked hopefully.

"No!" thundered Mr. Poulsen. "Not until, not until—" His face was turning red, and he turned toward the wall. He put his fist up over his head and let his forehead bump the wall. Then he seemed to talk to himself. "This is crazy. He's twelve years old. Younger than Keld, for crying out loud."

There was a sharp rap on the door, and Officer Pruneface stuck his head in. Peter wasn't glad to see him, but he was glad that something—anything—interrupted the nightmare.

"Aren't you done yet, Poulsen?" asked the officer. He smiled and winked at Mr. Poulsen. "I told you we'd finish first, so you lose the bet. We've already got the whole story out of the girl."

Peter's heart sank. Had Elise really told everything she knew?

"What did you do to my sister?" Peter pushed back his chair and stood up. He felt a flush of anger that he hadn't felt all night. "What did you do to her?"

"Oh, I see," sneered the officer. "We get a reaction out of this one now. Poulsen, I'll give you five more minutes before I come in and do it *my* way."

Officer Pruneface slammed the door, leaving Peter and Mr. Poulsen standing looking at each other.

"Look, don't you see it's too late to be a hero now?" Mr. Poulsen held out his arms with his hands up. "Your sister has already told us everything. So there's nothing left to win. The best you can do now is confirm her story—tell us the same thing—and those guys out there might leave her alone. You better do it now so you can both leave for home again. I'll try to get you off with just a warning to your parents. I promise you I'll do my best. What do you say?"

Peter chewed on his lip and thought he tasted a little blood.

He tried to think it through, using the last clear part of his brain. But all he could do was pray quietly while he stood staring at Mr. Poulsen. Peter wasn't at all sure that this man wasn't putting on an act, but he couldn't think straight. *Lord, what do I do?* he prayed, sinking down in the chair once more. *Should I give up and tell?*

Peter closed his eyes and thought about his sister, probably sitting in a little room like this, maybe with Officer Pruneface. And if what the officer had said was true, she had already told everything. He couldn't blame her, but then again, maybe these men weren't telling the truth. Maybe it was all an act and she was just sitting in another room like the one Peter was in, not saying a word. Or maybe . . .

Finally Peter opened his mouth, but nothing came out, not even a croak. When he forced his eyes back open, Mr. Poulsen was staring at him, shaking his head.

"You're too young for this," said the man. He stood up, pulled open the door, and motioned for Peter to come. He took Peter's arm and walked him down the hall to a flight of stairs. Everything was dark inside the large office building except for an occasional desk light. On one desk, piled high with papers, he glimpsed a clock in a small pool of light. One in the morning. They made their way up the stairs to the attic, the sixth floor.

By now Peter had figured out that the large building was shaped like a "U." Up in the attic, someone had added crude concrete block walls and narrow hallways. Mr. Poulsen led him past rows of plywood doors, each with ventilation holes drilled in the top and bottom and a small window covered by a plywood flap.

Then Peter remembered what he had overheard his friends at the Underground newspaper discussing: This was the prison the Germans had built on top of their headquarters as a way of keeping anyone from bombing the place—the same place the Underground kept asking the British to bomb and destroy.

At the end of the hallway, they turned right, passing several little doors. There were three toilets, a washroom with two dirty sinks, and a small room that looked like a kitchen. At the end of the hallway, a guard was sitting with his chin resting on his folded arms.

Mr. Poulsen stopped and cleared his throat loudly. The man in the chair popped up like a jack-in-the-box.

"I have one more for you tonight," said Mr. Poulsen. "Any more rooms in this hotel?"

The guard was an older man, with wisps of gray hair around the ears and wrinkles around his eyes. To Peter, he looked more like a shopkeeper or a baker than a soldier. When he stood up, he shook his head and his cheeks flapped, like a large dog with loose jowls.

"*Nein*. All twenty-two are full tonight." He nodded over to the other end of the hall. "Even the sister has one already. She's been asleep in there for an hour."

"Well then, put him in with that religious fanatic," said Mr. Poulsen. "He seems harmless enough."

The guard nodded and reached into his pocket for a large collection of keys. Only then did Mr. Poulsen release his grip on Peter's arm. It was firm but not as clawlike as Major Mueller's.

"We'll talk again in the morning," said Mr. Poulsen as the guard opened up the first door on the right for Peter. "I tried to help you, boy. Now you have to deal with Colonel Ludheim." He turned on his heel and disappeared.

Peter stumbled through the door, not knowing what more to expect of this bad dream, this prison, these people. He tumbled onto a bunk, one of two set up in the small, dark room, and covered his head with his hands. Only a little light filtered in from under the door and through the vent holes from the dim hallway. He hoped the person in the other bunk was asleep.

"Welcome to the Shell House," came a man's voice. It was the second person who had said that to him.

"Hi," Peter mumbled through his pillow. He tried to lower his voice so he didn't sound too much like a twelve-year-old.

"You're the first roommate I've had since I arrived," the man told him. "I'm Frank Nielsen."

By now Peter felt as if he were talking in his sleep, and perhaps he was. "I'm Peter Andersen. My sister's here too. Somewhere." He caught his breath, realizing he had just told the man his real name.

"Your sister's there across the hall, right?" asked Frank Nielsen.

"I'm not sure," Peter answered. "I don't know—"

"It's her. They brought her here about an hour ago." Then Peter heard a sigh. "Only I didn't know the Germans were putting kids in jail these days."

"You didn't hear her say anything?" whispered Peter.

"Not a thing," replied Frank. "But Colonel Ludheim, he was being his usual self. Completely obnoxious. I heard him tell her that since her brother had already told them everything, she just needed to cooperate. The usual lie."

"Say that again?" Peter rolled over onto his back and leaned closer to his new cellmate.

"I said, Colonel Ludheim was being his usual self. He's always playing games with prisoners' minds like that. Especially people who are new to the system."

"No, the part about me."

"Oh yes, he just said you had cooperated, and that if she did too, it would be much easier for you."

"But that's just what they told me!" Peter tried hard not to let his voice get above a whisper. "I didn't tell them anything yet."

Frank Nielsen chuckled. "I'm sure you didn't. It's how they do things here. Get you alone, and then tell you that everyone else is on their side now. Makes you feel as if you're the last one left in the entire world who isn't cooperating with them."

So Elise hasn't told anything either—at least, not yet. Peter tried to make sense of what the man had just told him. *Our friends at the newspaper are still safe . . . so far.*

But that was the only good thing he could think of. He curled up tighter and tried to block out the nightmare he was in, his ears buzzing as he nodded off. A moment later, Peter was asleep.

Prison Life

Just before Peter woke the next morning, he could hear the clanking sounds of doors being opened and closed, and the shuffling of people in the hall outside his door. Someone was shaking him, and he tried to turn over and cover his head.

"Leave me alone, Elise," he groaned. "Your turn to make breakfast this morning." That was his normal line when Elise tried to wake him. "Mom said it's your turn." Peter rolled over once more before he realized that his bed was different. It was hard, and the blanket was rough. This was definitely not his pillow, and it smelled like mothballs and mold. Where was he?

The person shaking Peter by the shoulders laughed softly. "I'm not Elise," said the voice. "But it *is* time to get up for some breakfast. It's seven-thirty, and you probably don't want to miss it. This is the only food you'll get before noon."

Peter rolled over, still not fully with it. Finally he realized he wasn't in his own bed at home, and it all came back to him—the day before, being taken by the soldiers, the ride in the back of the truck, Major Mueller and Mr. Poulsen trying to get him to talk . . .

"Tell me I'm not really here," Peter finally said. Frank Nielsen was still standing over him, patiently trying to wake him.

"You're not really here," said Frank. "Does that make you feel better? And the other thing is that if you don't get out of bed right now you're going to miss breakfast. Last chance."

Peter's stomach told him that he hadn't eaten since lunchtime yesterday, just before they had gone fishing with their grandfather. Suddenly that seemed like a long, long time ago. He sat up and looked around at the room they were in.

He had actually been in closets that were bigger. Between the two metal beds there was just enough room to stand, and then three feet to a plywood door. A small window cut into the top half of the door was big enough to pass a plate through. The walls were bleak and plain, and they didn't match the rest of the building. It looked as if this had been an attic at one time, and someone had decided to build a few walls in a hurry. And then there was Frank Nielsen, sitting on his neatly made bed.

Frank looked like a mailman, or a shopkeeper, or the man next door—except for his bright red, unkempt beard. He wore thick glasses and had a kind of smile that made his face look uneven. Still, he had a calm expression that kept Peter from panicking in the little space. Frank swept his hand around, like a chef introducing a new dinner.

"It's not much, but right now, this is home," he said. "I must admit, I've never had such a young roommate. How old are you? And what in the world are you doing in a place like this with all these troublemakers?"

"Everyone asks that," said Peter with a sigh. His stomach grumbled loudly. "I'm twelve."

"And you're hungry," said Frank as he reached under his mattress. He pulled out a small pocket watch, which he checked and then returned to its hiding place, and pointed at the opening in their door. "But it's seven thirty-two. They'll be opening the door just about—"

"Two plates!" someone grunted from the hallway as the little door swung open. A plate appeared, then another. Peter stood up to see what was happening.

"See?" said Frank as he pulled the plates into the little room. "I can set my watch by it. Lunch comes at noon, straight up, and dinner at five." He passed the first plate to Peter, and Peter tried not to make a face. It was a single small scoop of something that looked like oatmeal, but it was far thinner, and it smelled kind of greasy.

"Of course, the food's not anything to write home about, unless you want to make someone a little ill," continued Frank with his good-natured tone of voice. "But at least it's food." He sat down on the edge of his bunk, bowed his head for a moment, then looked up at Peter. "Why don't you sit down and enjoy the meal?"

Peter was still a little shocked, thinking that if he could just get back into bed and wake up again, this bad dream would go away. He sat down anyway.

"Want to pray for the meal?" the man asked, lifting his spoon.

Peter wasn't quite sure what to make of this man, but he was definitely different. What would it hurt?

"Okay, I guess," answered Peter. He recited the grace his father often said at home: "In Jesus' name we now with grateful hearts before thee bow, bless thou these gifts and grant that we may always thank and honor thee amen." He said it in one breath, the way his father always did.

"Amen." Frank looked up from his plate. "You learn that prayer at home? Where are you from?"

"Yeah," answered Peter, letting a little smile slip out. "We always said it at dinner. I'm from Helsingor, just like my sister. Well, obviously just like my sister. You really think she's across the hall?"

"From everything I heard last night before you showed up, yes, I'm sure," said Frank. "And I hate to say this, but this is not exactly a good place for a sister to be."

"I know." Peter nodded and pushed the food around on his

plate. "But it's not just her either. My un—" Peter was just about to tell the whole story of his Uncle Morten but changed his mind in midsentence. He bit his tongue and kept silent.

"You're already learning something about being in this prison," said Frank, his mouth half full. "It's good to watch your tongue. Actually, some of the finest men in Denmark are in these cells, not counting me. But you never know when you might run into a ringer. The Germans throw them in."

"A ringer?" asked Peter. He was finally getting up the courage—or rather the hunger—to take a bite of his food. "What's a ringer?"

"A Nazi informant, someone who works with the Nazis in secret. They get thrown in here to try and get information out of us by pretending to be prisoners. We know who they are mostly. They're pretty pathetic guys. But you better learn rule number one of surviving here: Never discuss anything about what got you here. With *anyone*." He pointed his spoon at Peter, then at himself. "And you can start practicing on me. I don't want to hear war stuff out of you, whatever your story is. And you must have some story for them to have put a twelve-year-old in this prison."

"I think they're just trying to show off or something," said Peter. His first bite wasn't as bad as he had thought it would be. The greasy porridge was simply tasteless. "Or maybe Major Mueller was in a bad mood."

"More than a bad mood." Frank put down his spoon. "In fact, this is about the craziest thing the Germans have ever done. Putting kids in prison! The war must be almost over."

Peter didn't exactly know how to respond, so he just kept eating. While they finished their meal, they chatted about their homes and families. Frank was married and had two small children, and he really was a mailman. That didn't explain his being in prison with the rest of the Resistance people, but Peter took the man's warning seriously. They would only talk about harmless things: families, homes, pets, travel, movie stars, records. Anything but the war.

"So you and your sister have homing pigeons?" Frank sounded interested. "I've always wondered how those birds did it. I mean, they make their way home from just about anywhere, right?"

Peter laughed, and it almost startled him. He hadn't imagined himself laughing in a place like this. "We think they have some kind of built-in compass," he explained. "Actually, one of the birds belongs to my friend Henrik, but he's a—"

Peter stopped suddenly. How could anybody have a normal conversation without getting into war-talk? The war touched everything.

"Uh-oh," said Frank. "He's a what? Or can't you tell me?"

Peter looked down at the floor and scraped his spoon around on the empty plate in his lap. "I think I can tell you this; it's nothing the Germans don't already know. He's a Jew. And he's not around anymore."

"Oh," replied Frank. "I'm sorry. I had some Jewish friends too. Only I didn't even know they were Jewish before it all happened."

There was another awkward silence, and Peter wondered if they had run out of things to say. Frank put down his plate and licked the spoon.

"But hey, let me tell you about a non-Jewish beagle I had back home," said Frank. "I actually trained him to sort mail."

"No, really?"

"Honest. I would put these big marks on the mail for my wife, and then tell the little dog to bring them to her. And he would only pick up the letters I had marked, if you can believe that. One by one he would pick them up in his little mouth and trot them over to her."

Peter laughed once more. He hadn't expected the prison's "religious fanatic" to be a funny mailman.

"That's great," said Peter. "Elise would love to hear that. She's always been the one who wanted a dog or a cat, but we live in an apartment."

"Well, I should meet this sister of yours," said Frank, standing up on his bed. "Let's at least find out for sure where she's at."

"How do we do that?" Peter put down his plate and watched his cellmate grab a small ledge next to the ceiling and hoist himself up to a set of small ventilation holes.

"Hey," Frank whispered into the holes. "Pass along a message, would you? My cellmate has a sister here in the hotel, and he wants to say hello. He also wants to know where she is and how she's doing. Pass it on."

Frank swung back down and sat on his bunk.

"Now we just wait for the telegraph message to come back. Depends on how bored people are at the moment, and if all the rooms are full, but we can usually pass a message around and back all the way through in five minutes. We're at the end here. There are about twenty other rooms. Remember, I'm a mailman, so I know these things."

While they were waiting, Peter explored the room. It was like a little wooden box, nailed together by someone who wasn't very good with a hammer and nails. The corners didn't quite fit together, and cold drafts reached in from all sides. Peter looked up at his new roommate.

"Not much of a prison, is it?" he asked.

Frank scratched his red beard and looked around. "No, you're right about that. The Germans put it up in a hurry. But I guess it does the job. At least the company isn't so bad."

"You know everybody here?"

"Just about. I'm pretty good at names."

Should I ask? Peter wondered. Maybe Frank would know about Uncle Morten . . .

"So have you ever heard of anyone named Morten?" Peter finally got up his courage to ask. "Morten Andersen?"

"Friend of yours?"

"No—yes—I mean . . ." Peter decided he would take a chance. "He's my uncle, and I thought he might be in here too."

"Well, wouldn't that be something!" Frank leaned back and

smiled. "Uncle and nephew in the same prison." Then he studied Peter's serious face for a moment and wrinkled his brows. "I'm sorry, Peter. I didn't mean to make it a joke." He shook his head slowly. "I don't know of anybody here named Morten. I'm sorry."

Peter's face fell, and he closed his eyes for a moment. *I should have known*, he told himself. *Uncle Morten must be somewhere else.*

A whisper from up near the ceiling made Peter look up. Frank nodded at Peter. "You answer the phone this time. It's for you."

Peter hoisted himself up as he had seen Frank do and put his face up to the set of small, round holes. "Hello?" he whispered, not knowing quite what to say. This wasn't a telephone really.

"The sister's in number two. She's fine. Alone. Says hi. Hasn't talked to anybody yet. That's all."

Peter felt a wave a relief to hear from Elise. Even if he couldn't find out anything about his uncle, Elise was still okay!

"Thanks," Peter whispered back, wondering how he should "hang up." But Frank was yanking on his ankle, and Peter came tumbling down on his cellmate's bunk just as the door swung slowly open. Another prisoner stepped in to collect their plates as a bored-looking guard stood outside.

"I forgot to tell you," said Frank, after the door had closed again. "When somebody comes to the door, you better get down from the telephone holes quick. The Germans don't like us chatting too much."

"Okay," said Peter, looking back up at the four small holes in the wall. "But I got the message about my sister."

"Yeah? That's great. What did she say?"

"She's okay, I guess. Room two."

"That's practically straight across the hall," explained Frank. "If you yelled, she would probably hear you. But—" He put up his finger. "I don't recommend doing that."

Peter moved to his own bunk and leaned back, wondering how often he would be able to pass a message to Elise. Of course, what else was there to say? He just wanted to be in the same

room, to be able to talk, really talk. *Elise, all alone!* At least he had
Frank to talk to here.

"What else do you guys talk about?" Peter wondered, putting
his hands behind his head.

"Oh, the food. We warn each other about things the guards
are doing. Mostly we try to keep each other from giving up—kind
of encourage each other. Then every once in a while in the morn-
ings, someone asks me for a Bible verse." He chuckled. Everyone
thinks I'm the prison chaplain."

"You're the only one with a Bible?"

"That's me. Someone left this little pocket version here. I
found it under the mattress when I got here three weeks ago."

Sure enough, a whisper came from the next cell about twenty
minutes later, and Frank looked up from where he was reading.
He smiled at Peter and stood up on his bunk.

"Watch this—they'll be asking for the verse. I'll give them the
one I was reading yesterday before you got here. From Isaiah."

Frank stood on the edge of his bed, reading from his Bible,
while Peter watched the mailman-turned-preacher.

"Here's one for you," Frank whispered through the ventilation hole. "Listen: 'Fear not, for I have redeemed you; I have
called you by name; you are mine.' Are you listening?" Frank
waited for the man in the next cell to respond before he continued
reading. "Okay, here's the rest: 'When you pass through the waters, I will be with you; and when you pass through the rivers,
they will not sweep over you. When you walk through the fire,
you will not be burned; the flames will not set you ablaze.' That's
from Isaiah forty-three."

The voice next door mumbled something Peter didn't catch.

"There's always more where that came from," answered
Frank. Then he hopped down and glanced at his cellmate.

"Ever heard that one before?" he asked Peter.

Peter hadn't, and he shook his head. Still, there was something very familiar about the words. Passing through the waters;
he had done that before. He hadn't explained the whole story of

how he and his sister had helped their friend Henrik row across the water to Sweden, though. Peter hugged his knees tightly and closed his eyes as he thought about the last part of the verse Frank had read. *The waters have been bad enough. I hope I don't have to walk into the flames too.*

BUNDLE OF FUR

By Tuesday night, Peter had learned all about prison routine. There were the hourly checks by the guards, but not much of anything else. During that afternoon, Peter counted the guards going by eight times.

"Why hasn't anyone come to ask me more questions?" Peter wondered aloud.

"Who knows?" answered Frank. "It's crazy enough that the Nazis are keeping you here. They probably think they're teaching you some kind of lesson."

"Yeah, but for three days? And what about my sister?"

"You're asking the wrong person, Peter. I wish I knew what to tell you. But I'll tell you one thing—you can be glad you haven't been interrogated like the men around here."

Peter nodded. He had noticed some of the bruises on Frank's face and arms.

"Ready to memorize another section of Isaiah?" asked Frank.

"You know I've never done this before," Peter told him. "I'm not sure if I can do any more verses."

"Never memorized the Bible?" Frank acted as if every Danish

boy would have done such a thing.

"Actually, no," admitted Peter. "Not until now."

"Well, I wouldn't wish this prison on anybody, but it's a good thing you ran into me."

"Maybe you're right, Mr. Preacher. So go ahead. Quiz me."

Frank flipped the pages of his well-worn book to the Old Testament. "Okay, you asked for it. Chapter fifty-five. The part about the rain."

Peter shook his head. He had surprised himself; he had actually enjoyed all the hours spent memorizing with Frank. It almost made him feel guilty, wondering what Elise was going through all alone. "I can't believe I've actually memorized this," he said. "Back home, I hardly even open my Bible. Guess when there's nothing else to do . . ."

"Maybe we should be stuck in prison more often," suggested Frank with a grin.

"Well, I don't know about that."

"No, I don't either."

"Okay then, here we go." Peter twirled the hair on his forehead around his finger, concentrating. "I remember this part: 'As the rain and the snow come down from heaven, so is my word that goes out from my mouth: It will not return to me empty—' "

"Hey, whoa." Frank put up his hand. "You skipped a few lines."

Peter looked puzzled, then searched his memory once more. "Take it easy, Frank. I told you I've never done this before."

Frank smiled, the patient teacher in a prison cell. "You can memorize it. Just imagine the words on the page. Then close your eyes and read them. But how about if you tell me what it means first?"

Peter thought for a minute, then shrugged. "I'm not sure. I get the part about the rain, but the rest, I'm not sure."

"Want me to explain? What I—"

Frank stopped what he was saying when he heard the sound of boots marching down the hall. A dragging or shuffling sound meant that a prisoner was coming too. But there was none of that; the footsteps stopped in front of their door, and Peter heard the sound of a key turning.

"Get up!" announced a young guard, poking his head into the room. "The kid. Right now!" Another guard stood out in the hallway with his rifle drawn. The first guard pointed at Peter and motioned with his hand.

"Don't make me wait," he growled.

Peter looked over at Frank, wondering if this was normal. But his cellmate could only reach over and pat him on the shoulder.

"We'll finish the Sunday school lesson later," said Frank. "Just don't forget the verse."

The guard's voice was urgent, as if something were about to happen. So Peter followed the two guards out into the hallway, while Frank finished his verse back in the cell. Peter could hear the muffled voice.

" . . . it will not return to me empty, but will accomplish what I desire and achieve the purpose for which I sent it."

Peter listened for more, but Frank was finished. Next to him, the young guard looked nervously up and down the hallway, while the other one locked the cell door behind them.

"Okay," said the first guard. "All clear. See you in the morning."

The guard with the rifle simply nodded and disappeared down the hall, leaving Peter and the young man in the plain gray uniform alone. By the light of a bare bulb hanging in the hallway, Peter looked at the numbers on each door. The guard seemed distracted as he paused at a small table to fill out several papers. Maybe this would be Peter's chance to see if Elise was okay.

"Hey," said Peter, looking over at the guard. The teenager had a gun in his holster, but it wasn't drawn. He glanced up from his paper work with an annoyed expression.

"*Ein Minutten*," said the guard, holding up a finger. "One minute."

"While you're doing that," said Peter, "can't I at least say hello to my sister? She's right across the hall."

Again the guard looked around nervously, then he scribbled something quickly on the paper, and waved Peter off as if he were a fly. "Who?" he asked.

"My sister," Peter replied. "You know, *meine Schwester*?" Peter had learned a little more German during the last semester in school. The guard just looked as if he wanted to get rid of Peter.

"*Ja, ja*," said the guard. "But just for a minute, and only through the window. Come on, *schnell*—hurry."

Peter didn't wait for the guard to change his mind, and he had no idea why the man was going to let him see Elise. The guard unlatched the small window in a door across the hall and peered in. Then he pointed at Peter. "One minute," he warned.

Peter stepped up to the door and got up on his tiptoes to see in. There was Elise, looking very, very tired, sitting on a plain bed just like his. Peter knocked on the door to get her attention. She looked up slowly, with a scared look on her face. But she smiled when she saw who it was.

"Peter!" she said, rushing to the door. She took his hand through the opening. "What are you doing here?"

"I don't know, but I'm okay," he said. "Did they do anything to you?"

"No, I'm just bored out of my mind, sitting here staring at the walls," she answered back. "I think I started talking to myself. I was talking to some bugs on the floor too. But I'm fine, mostly. Colonel Pruneface got purple in the face at me the other night, trying to make me say something." Then she looked down and lowered her voice to a whisper. "He told me you told them everything and—"

"They gave me the same story about you," Peter whispered back, hoping the guard wouldn't overhear them. "But there's this other guy in my cell—Frank—he's really nice. Frank says they always try that on people just to get them to talk, but I haven't told them anything at all. Listen, they're taking me somewhere again, so I won't say anything as long as you don't. If—"

"Time's up. Let's go," announced the guard, stepping up to the door. Peter gripped his sister's hand even tighter, and she squeezed his hand back.

"It's okay," whispered Elise. "Dad will find us soon."

Without a word the guard yanked Peter's hand out of the little door, slammed the door shut in Elise's face, and led Peter down the corridor.

"I don't know why I let you do that," said the guard. "If Colonel Ludheim had come walking down the hall just then, it would not have been pleasant."

Peter didn't say anything. He felt himself steered down several dim hallways, then down some stairs to the floor below, then through a large, open office. He thought he had been in the same office before, or at least marched through it. Peter turned around for a moment.

"Where are you taking me?" he asked the guard.

"Shut up," answered the young soldier, giving Peter a shove on the shoulder to keep him going. Everything was quiet, except for the sound of someone Peter assumed was a janitor rummaging through trash cans in an office. One of the metal cans fell with a clang, and it sounded like a pile of boxes falling to the floor.

"Who's there?" said the guard, peering nervously around the corner into the dark office. He unsnapped his gun holster and pulled out a long, menacing German army pistol. Then he glanced back at Peter for a moment, as if he couldn't make up his mind whether to investigate or stay with his prisoner.

"I said, who's there?" The young guard waved his pistol at the darkened room, but there was no reply. Peter wasn't sure whether he should hide behind the guard, or escape to a closet. Another trash can tumbled, and Peter jumped behind a desk.

In the next ten seconds, Peter heard someone scurrying around, playing tag in the dark. The guard shouted a warning, and then there was some kind of scuffle. Peter burrowed headfirst under the desk, while the guard ran circles around the office.

"Halt!" shouted the man, but the scuffling only got nearer to the desk. A moment later, something jumped in next to Peter, and Peter bumped his head trying to jump out.

"Yow!" Peter hollered, doing everything he could to get away from the phantom that was now scratching and spitting in his face. Something pounced onto the back of Peter's shirt, and claws locked into his skin. There was a shrill scream in his ear as he yelled in pain.

Peter reached around to unlatch whatever was hooked onto his back and came up with a handful of fur. It bit his hand, and this time Peter knew he had to get this wild animal off his back. He yanked hard, ripping his shirt as he did, and held on to the clawing bundle of fur.

Now he could feel that it wasn't very big, only a small animal. Peter took hold of what he thought was the scruff of its neck and held the creature out in front of him. Someone finally found the main lights, and Peter blinked as he climbed out from under the desk.

"What's all the racket here?" came a loud voice, one that sounded vaguely familiar. Peter looked away from his squirming, clawing catch for a moment to look at who had come into the office. Keld Poulsen's father was standing there in a rumpled suit with his arms crossed, looking much the same as he had three nights before.

"Herr Poulsen," said the young guard. He was standing by the light switch, his gun still drawn. "I was just taking this kid to interrogation when we heard a noise."

Mr. Poulsen surveyed the mess in the office, with trash cans and papers strewn all over the floor. It looked like a small hurricane had just swept through. Then he saw Peter, who was still trying to keep the kitten from scratching his arms. He grinned for a moment.

"You again! Well, it looks as if you've found a friend," said Mr. Poulsen. "I don't know how it got in, especially all the way up here." Then he gave the guard a tired look. "All this commotion from a little striped cat? Why don't you just return to your post. I'll take care of the boy."

"I'm sorry, Mr. Poulsen. I can't let you do that. Colonel Ludheim asked me to deliver him directly to the interrogation station. I would at least have to check in with him first." He hesitated before replacing the pistol in his holster.

"You let me take care of the colonel," replied Mr. Poulsen. "I'll make sure everything is done according to form, and no one will hear of this little incident about a soldier with a drawn gun chasing a cat. On the other hand"—he scratched his chin—"it might make an amusing story."

Peter could tell his young guard didn't need a lot of convincing. With a last glance at the wrecked office, the guard turned on his heel. "He's all yours, Herr Poulsen," he called back.

Mr. Poulsen looked at Peter and grinned. "Come with me," he said. "And bring your cat. We're going to have another one of our talks."

Peter was almost out of the room when something made him glance back over his shoulder once more. He caught a glimpse of Mr. Poulsen giving the guard a sly grin and a thumb and finger okay sign, but Peter quickly turned back before anyone saw him looking. They continued downstairs, then to one of the many wood-paneled offices on the lower floor.

"So, here we are." Mr. Poulsen settled back into a black leather chair. The windows in this office looked out to the dark courtyard. "Here we are once more."

Peter sat nervously in another chair, the cat in his lap. He was afraid to let go of the animal, and the large kitten even seemed to be getting used to Peter. *At least it's not scratching my back off anymore,* thought Peter.

"You have a pet at home in Helsingor?" asked Mr. Poulsen. Peter could tell he was going to try the Mr. Friendly approach again. Peter shook his head, and Mr. Poulsen leaned forward in the chair to stare at Peter. The man loosened his tie.

"Look, you've been through a lot," said Mr. Poulsen. "If you were my son, I'd be afraid for you, I would." Then he looked around the office, got to his feet, walked over to an outside door, and swung it open. A cold blast of air hit Peter in the face.

"All right, I want to show you that I'm serious about what I'm saying. So you're free to go." He looked at Peter for a moment for effect, then pointed at the open door. "I haven't even cleared this with Colonel Ludheim, but yes, you're free to go. You can even take that cat with you if you like. Go on. I'm serious."

Peter sat quietly, scratching the cat behind the ears. By now, it was purring.

"You don't believe me, do you?" Mr. Poulsen walked over to Peter and pulled him to his feet. "I said you were free to go, and now all you do is sit there, silent as a stone. It looks as if you actually want to stay! But me? I meant what I said, and all I ask in return is just a little bit of information."

Peter knew it was coming. *Just a little bit of information*, Peter thought. *Next he's going to take out a piece of paper, make it easy for me to tell everything I know about our friends at the newspaper. "Just write it down here," he'll tell me.*

"I thought you already had all the information you needed from my sister." Peter crossed his arms and set his jaw.

The man shook his head and smiled. "What? Oh. Just need to confirm it," he said. "It's a simple matter."

Mr. Poulsen pulled a notebook and pencil from his pocket and laid them on a small table in front of Peter.

"Look," he said. "You don't need to say a word, so if anyone ever asks, you can say you never said a word, right?" He smiled once more, and Peter thought he was going to get sick to his stomach. This time there was no confusion in Peter's mind about Keld's father. No, this man was just like his son. Peter didn't believe a word he was saying. Every smile meant something sinister.

"So you write, and I'll just ask you a few questions," continued Mr. Poulsen. "You can even pretend you're in school doing an exam, okay?" Another phony smile.

Peter looked at the notebook and rolled the pencil between his fingers in one hand. In the other, the kitten was squirming around again, wanting to get down. Mr. Poulsen looked pleased.

"That's better," said the man. "Help us out here, and I'll see to it that you can keep the kitten. Would you like that? Just write down a couple of things, and you and your sister will be on your way and out of here in a matter of minutes. See your parents again. I'll even call them for you. The door is open to you, remember?" He reached over and pushed it shut. "But I'll just have to close it here for a moment to keep out the cold, right?" He laughed again, nervously, and continued his instructions.

"Now here's what I'd like you to do. First write down the names of all the people you know who were working on the illegal newspaper. Got it? If you don't know the names, you can write down what they looked like. Color of hair, eyeglasses, that sort of thing. You could even draw a picture of their faces if you like. Think back to whatever nicknames you might have heard them use, or anything you might have heard them say. Got it? I'll give you a couple of minutes for that."

Peter paused over the pencil, then started to draw. First he outlined a woman with a long dress, puffy short sleeves, and shoulder-length black hair. Next, he added seven smaller figures gathered around her. Under the woman, he wrote "Snow White." He turned the notebook so Mr. Poulsen couldn't stare directly at what he was doing.

"Should I draw more than one?" Peter asked, giving the man his best defeated look.

"More than one, of course, of course." Mr. Poulsen rubbed his hands together in delight.

So Peter continued with his drawings, giving them little hats, brooms, and pickaxes. The Seven Dwarfs. Some had big noses, and one had those big, floppy ears. It was crazy, but he tried hard to keep from smiling. He knew for certain that Mr. Poulsen would come unglued when he saw. Peter put down his pencil and scratched the kitten's ears. He could feel his heart pounding in his own ears.

"Finished already?" asked Mr. Poulsen. "Good. Now, write down anything you know about where they live or work. Did they ever mention their jobs? Their neighborhoods? Whether they could walk home? Anything is good information to include. Anything at all can help."

Peter pretended to concentrate for a moment, chewing the end of the pencil. When he and Elise had gone to see the movie *Snow White and the Seven Dwarfs*, it had been their favorite. That was just before the war started, but Peter could still see the moving cartoon when he closed his eyes. He wrote down a few lines under the drawings: "They whistle a lot and live in a little cottage in the woods. I think they work in a mine." This was getting a little outrageous, Peter knew, but he had to follow through on the Snow White theme. He was committed now.

"Very good," said Mr. Poulsen. "Now for the last question, I want you to concentrate very hard, and then we'll be all done for today. This is very important, now. Tell me everything you know about the illegal newspaper. Who runs it? Where is it now? How do you pass it out? Who passes out the paper? What are their names?"

Peter thought for a minute longer. He was in over his head now. Finally he printed as many names as he could remember: Dopey, Sneezy, Sleepy, Grumpy, Doc, and then he forgot the rest. In big letters across the bottom he wrote, "They all run the newspaper." He signed his name in the corner and closed the notebook, then closed his eyes. Would Mr. Poulsen kill him on the spot?

Mr. Poulsen, the flash of victory in his eyes, reached over and took the notebook off the table. "You've done the right thing, my boy, the right thing for your country." He patted Peter on the head and motioned for him to stand up.

"I hope so," said Peter. *Maybe Mr. Poulsen won't read it until I get back to my cell,* he wished. More than that, he wished he could hide somewhere far away from this man, somewhere safe.

"Now, I know without looking that all this information is accurate," beamed Mr. Poulsen. "I just know you're that kind of person. But I must tell you that some of the boys here get pretty upset if they get information that doesn't match reality." He smiled, but not too sweetly. "I think you're old enough to know what that means. Now, I must be—"

A rap at the door interrupted the man.

"Yes?" Mr. Poulsen reached to unbolt the door to the hallway.

"Poulsen, are you still playing games in there?" It was Colonel Ludheim, rattling the doorknob.

"Well, come in, my dear colonel," said Mr. Poulsen. "We've just been having a most constructive chat with our young visitor here." He finished unbolting the door and swung it open for Colonel Ludheim.

"Constructive?" asked the colonel, stepping into the room. "How constructive is that?"

"I believe you'll find some information here," said Mr. Poulsen, holding out the notebook with a flourish. Peter was starting to wish he had just left it blank. Maybe it would have been better to still have Mr. Poulsen digging at him, trying to get him to talk. In a moment, the colonel would read his words, and Peter was sure of one thing: He was not going to laugh. The colonel started leafing through the notebook while Mr. Poulsen kept up his nervous chatter.

"Only three simple questions to answer, Colonel Ludheim. It was simple." Mr. Poulsen chirped and walked around the table as if he had just bagged a prize goose. Colonel Ludheim scratched his chin and looked back at Mr. Poulsen with a curious expression. Peter tried to sink under the table.

"And what were those questions, Mr. Poulsen?" asked the colonel. The veins in his neck seemed to stand out. "Did they have anything to do with cartoon characters?"

Mr. Poulsen's face was one big question mark, and Colonel Ludheim flung the notebook at his face.

"You fool!" cried Colonel Ludheim. "If we want a job done right, we have to give it to a German every time!" The German officer glanced over his shoulder and called to a guard in the hallway behind him. "Corporal! Take this child back to detention immediately. Herr Poulsen and I need to have a short training session."

"Yes, sir!" snapped the soldier from the hallway. He stepped into the room and took Peter by the arm, roughly. Peter tried to keep the small cat curled up like a football under his other arm.

"But, Colonel, sir," objected Mr. Poulsen. "The boy has a cat. I was going to—"

"Yes," interrupted Colonel Ludheim, "and a lively imagination as well." The German officer didn't even look at Peter. "Here, read this, Poulsen, and you'll see how this twelve-year-old makes a monkey out of you."

The door slammed behind him, and as Peter was briskly taken away toward the stairs, he could still hear Colonel Ludheim lecturing Mr. Poulsen.

"So! Before you go taking on any more assignments on your own, Poulsen, I'm going to teach you a thing or two about interrogation—a concept you don't seem to understand very well. And another thing, I had a guard bringing this boy directly to the interrogation center, and you have no authority whatever to change the procedure." Peter could tell the colonel was just warming up.

"I'm sorry, Colonel," mumbled Mr. Poulsen. "It won't happen again. . . ."

The guard gave Peter's arm a tug as they headed back up the stairs.

"Let's go," growled the guard.

Peter didn't answer, just did his best to keep up without falling down the stairs. For the last few steps, he was dragged by the collar and dumped into his cell.

"Back again so soon?" asked Frank. He was lying in the same spot as when Peter had left him.

"Yeah, I'm back," replied Peter. "And look what I found." He held up the young cat for his cellmate to see. "Or actually, look who found me."

Frank put down his book and stared. Then he chuckled, shook his head, and reached out to pet the animal. "Are you going to tell me how this happened?"

Peter told him the entire story, not leaving out any details.

"I knew that all along about Poulsen," said Frank, after Peter had finished. "The Nazis use him as a kind of gentle guy, the front man, to try to get information out of us. He always acts as if he wants to do us some kind of favor, like he's on our side, but—"

"But he's really not, is he?" asked Peter. "I feel sorry for him."

"He's a sad character," agreed Frank. "But that looks like quite a cat you've got there. They let you keep it?"

Peter shrugged. "First Mr. Poulsen said I could keep it as long as I told him what he wanted to know. Then when I didn't tell, he tried to explain to the colonel, but the colonel was hopping mad at him by that time. Wouldn't let him say anything. So I got sent away, and here I am."

"Of course, someone's going to catch on pretty soon. About the cat, I mean."

"But at least we can keep kitty for a while," said Peter. "He looked lost, like he needed a home. He just scared me for a minute. And that guard too."

"I'll say," laughed Frank. "Lost on the third floor of the Shell House—Gestapo headquarters and Nazi prison for famous Underground troublemakers and wayward children. That cat was about as lost as they come. Got a name for him?"

Peter thought for a moment, trying to come up with an ideal name. The kitten was exploring under his bunk, batting a dust ball.

"I don't know," Peter finally said. "My sister was always the one to come up with names. She named all our pigeons back home. I wish I could ask her."

"Well, maybe you can," suggested Frank. "It's almost time for the evening message."

Peter looked at him blankly, waiting for Frank to explain.

"Oh, I haven't told you about that, have I?" He sat up, looking for the cat. "You already know how we pass messages, but you've fallen asleep early these last two nights. We do this message every evening at the same time so that people can have something to look forward to. It helps us make sure everyone is keeping out of trouble."

"Okay," said Peter. "So can we send Elise a message?"

"I think so," answered Frank. "Let's just see if anyone is up and around." He stood on his bed and pulled himself up to the ventilation holes. "Hey, neighbor," Peter heard him whisper. "Got a message for you. Can you pass it along?"

Frank waited for a moment, then put his ear to the holes and nodded. "Okay," he whispered once more. "Here it is, and it's for the little girl they're holding across the hall. Yes, I said little girl. Got it? Here it is: Her brother got a cat. Yes, I said a cat. . . . What? C-A-T. You learned to spell that a long time ago. That's what I said. Four legs, catches mice, that sort of thing. Never mind, just pass the message. Yeah, let me start again. Brother got a cat. Needs a name for it. Please advise. . . . That's all, okay? Thanks, we'll wait."

Peter smiled at the thought of his message being passed along from cell to cell.

"Now we just have to wait for a few minutes," said Frank as he jumped down. "Hopefully everybody is in tonight or the connection can't go through all the way to your sister's room. Know what I mean?"

Peter nodded, and they sat down to wait. Frank pulled out an old crossword puzzle, which he held up to the hallway light coming in from a crack in the door.

"I've been through these puzzles about a hundred times already," mumbled Frank. "Maybe you want to take a look." Peter leaned over and tried to read the page. It was already scribbled over, and the pages were dog-eared from use. Peter squinted to read an unfamiliar word.

"Hey," said Peter in disgust. "This is a German crossword puzzle."

Frank just shrugged. "Better than nothing, don't you think?" He didn't wait for an answer. "Here's a good one," Frank said, looking up with a smile. "What's a nine-letter word for 'place of criminals'?"

Peter scratched his head, trying to remember the German word for prison.

"Nine letters? Really?" he asked.

"Would I kid you? Nine letters."

"Can't we just put in the Danish word?" asked Peter. "It's probably G-E-something, and I'm tired of trying to think in German. Why don't we—" Peter felt a sneeze coming on just then. "Why don't we just put in . . . ah . . . put in—"

Just then Peter let loose with a hurricane of a sneeze, capped off by a stomping of his feet.

"*Gesundheit!*" said Frank.

Peter looked up from wiping his face on his sleeve. "See what I mean? Don't say that!"

"Don't say what?" Frank was puzzled.

"You know, 'Gesundheit.' I'm sick of all those German words."

"Oh, sorry. I guess that means you don't want to do the crossword anymore?"

Peter had to laugh as he tried to get comfortable in his bunk. "I'm sorry, Frank," he told his roommate. "I don't mean to be so grouchy."

"Not a problem. I shouldn't be sitting around here anyway." He stood up and started stretching. "I should be doing my exercises."

After Frank finished stretching, he started running in place. Finally Peter stood up to join him, even though there was barely enough floor space for both of them to stand at one time.

"Yes, join me, by all means." Frank smiled.

Peter joined in the exercise. He went faster and faster, trying to chase away the gloomy feeling that kept tugging at him. If he let it take over, he would only start crying again. Still, he couldn't help thinking about home, about his mom and dad and about them worrying, about Elise all alone in a prison cell. Being in this prison wasn't quite what Peter had expected. He ran even faster, until he thought he would drop. He was making so much racket that he didn't hear whispering from the ventilation holes.

"Hey, did you hear that?" asked Frank.

Peter stopped for breath. "What? Hear what?"

"Psst," came their neighbor's voice. "Message from your sister."

Peter sprang up on Frank's bunk to get the message.

"Sorry," Peter apologized. "I didn't hear you."

"No, obviously you didn't." He sounded a little put out that Peter hadn't "answered the phone" right away. Frank had said the man was a banker in real life—kind of crabby. "Your sister says that if you ever get a cat you should name him Tiger Lily or Snow White, depending on what color he is. And what kind of a message is that?"

"Uh, I don't know." Peter didn't know how to explain his cat, and it was obvious Elise didn't quite understand the message either. "That's okay. That's fine. Thanks."

"So what do we name the little beast?" Frank asked when Peter sat down on his bunk. Peter reached around and picked up the frisky little animal while Frank poured some water into his hand from a bottle on the shelf. The cat eagerly lapped up the liquid.

"She didn't quite get it," reported Peter, "but she said that if I ever got a cat, I should name it Tiger Lily or Snow White, depending on the cat's color."

"So we know which name fits better."

Peter looked the young cat in the eye and scratched his ear.

"What do you think?" Peter asked the cat. "My sister says we should name you Tiger Lily. But you don't look like a lily to me, so how about just Tiger, huh?"

As if he understood, the kitten turned his head toward Peter and gave a squeaky little roar. Peter and Frank laughed.

"Tiger must suit you fine, little guy," said Peter. He put the cat back down on the floor, and Tiger disappeared under the bed while Peter settled down for the evening. He dangled his hand over the edge, and Tiger came up to attack a finger.

"Catch a mouse tonight, Tiger," he whispered over the side of the bunk. "You're not going to like the oatmeal in the morning. Course, neither am I."

Peter pulled up the thin blanket around his shoulders, shivered, and tried to remember what day it was. *What happened to Grandpa, Mom, and Dad? Why haven't they found us yet? How is Elise doing all by herself?* He fought tears but eventually gave up. He wouldn't let Frank hear him crying, though, so he covered his face with the blanket and tried to sleep.

But he just couldn't. He kept thinking about the conversation he had overheard about the British coming to bomb the prison—the very prison in which he now found himself a prisoner. *The British are going to bomb us, probably. Right here. And I can't tell anyone, not even Frank.*

If he could only get to sleep, he thought, the time would pass more quickly. Then when he woke up, his father would be standing at the door of this little room, ready to take him and Elise home. The colonel would come and apologize for the inconvenience. It had all been a mistake, he would say. There had never been any Underground newspaper. The British had decided to bomb some other target, he would say. The war is over, he would tell them, so please have a good day. *Wouldn't it be nice?*

————

The sound of rough German voices out in the hall pulled Peter halfway out of a dream a few hours later. Confused, he listened in the darkness, not understanding who they were or where he was. He lay stiffly on his hard bed, sniffling and shivering. *Maybe I'm still dreaming*, Peter thought.

"One of these days you're going to tell us what we need to know," someone yelled gruffly. "There was nothing in your apartment. Do you hear me? Nothing except a lot of old books. Books about God, no less!" The German voice snorted. "No addresses, no names, no nothing."

There was the sound of tumbling and then the slam of a door as someone was pushed into another one of the cells. It could have been two doors down the hall, maybe three, but Peter was still only half aware of what was going on. Then the German voice spoke up again. "What are you, Andersen, some kind of priest? Go ahead and pray, then!"

Peter heard an evil laugh, but this time his eyes snapped open at the mention of his name. *Andersen!* He felt his heart beating wildly, and he almost jumped out of his bed.

If that's Uncle Morten, thought Peter, *I could just yell. Maybe he would hear me.*

Yeah, and then what? He answered his own question. *I'll just get him in more trouble. Maybe they would even use me to get at him—like torture me until he tells them what they want.* Peter's mind had jump-started, and now it was racing.

Outside his own door, Peter could hear the guard, the same one who had been laughing and yelling at Andersen, whoever that was. The smoke from the man's cigarette stung Peter's eyes, and Peter could hear him pacing up and down the hall in front of his room. After a while, the guard dragged a chair from down the hall and sat down.

Maybe he'll fall asleep, and then I can yell to see if it's really Uncle Morten. Peter might have taken the chance, but the guard got up again and started whistling in the dark. Only a faint light filtered in through the cracks of his cell and under the door. Peter had no idea what time it was. It felt very late.

KEEPING SECRETS

Peter tried desperately to stay awake. But the next thing he knew, Tiger was standing on his stomach and kneading it like dough. The cat's claws dug through Peter's shirt.

"Hey, you're a little alarm clock," Peter yawned. Frank was already sitting up on the bunk next to him, rubbing the sleep out of his eyes.

"You've been sleeping late too," Frank told him. "It's almost breakfast time."

Peter couldn't believe he had slept so well, not after what had happened the night before. Tiger jumped off his bed and disappeared under Frank's.

"Frank, you won't believe what I heard last night!" Peter sat up in bed and tried to explain what he'd heard during the night. Most of what he remembered was kind of hazy, and he was having a hard time with all the details.

"Sounds like quite a dream," commented Frank. He scratched his chin.

"But it wasn't a dream," Peter insisted. "I woke up—well, I kind of woke up—and heard this guard out in the hallway. I didn't recognize the voice. But they were calling someone Andersen, and they were mad because they had searched this man's apartment and hadn't found anything."

"They searched his apartment?" Frank looked at Peter with a puzzled expression. "That means something to you?"

Peter's shoulders slumped. "Oh, I never told you about my uncle's apartment. It was ransacked. Well, anyway, if it *is* him, he's just down the hallway. I could yell and he would hear me."

Frank's expression turned serious, and he raised a finger to his lips. "I wouldn't do that," he warned in a hushed voice. "Even if it is your uncle, it won't do him any good to know you're here. And if the Germans find out, they'll just use that against him. You need to keep quiet about this. We can check around. We can find out, but you can't do something stupid."

"Of course I want to find out!" Peter scratched his head and sat up. Tiger was playing with something under Frank's bunk, and Peter reached down to see what it was.

"What have you got there, Tiger?" he asked, grabbing what looked like a piece of string out of the cat's mouth. It felt soft, and then Peter realized what it was.

"Gross!" said Peter, holding up the mouse tail for Frank to see. "Look, Frank."

"Not bad," Frank nodded. "Looks like your little Tiger knows how to take care of himself. You'll have a good mouser to take home with you."

"Take home?"

"Of course." Frank stood up and straightened the thin blanket on his bed. "I'm sure you and your sister will be out of here today, tomorrow at the latest. I've never seen such a crazy thing—the Germans holding children as prisoners. And you're going to have to take that cat with you, I guarantee."

Just then a key rattled in their door. Frank dropped to the floor and pushed the cat farther under his bunk. Tiger must have thought it was a great game and batted the mouse tail out for Frank to play with.

"Knock it off under there!" Frank whispered as the door creaked open. The guard only gave Frank a curious look as he checked inside the room. Then he turned to Peter and jerked his head, motioning for the boy to come with him.

As Peter stuck his feet into his shoes, he looked down in time to see Tiger crawling out from under the bed and Frank trying to stuff him back under. The cat was having a wonderful time and came charging out the other side. Peter slipped out as fast as he could while the guard shut and locked the door.

Peter marched in front of the man on the same route he had taken before, down the hallway to the corner stairway, down to the third floor, and through another large office area. He tried to ignore his queasy stomach.

The guard knocked on a large paneled door, then poked his head inside. "Sir, I'm here with the kid."

"What took you so long?" boomed a familiar, unpleasant voice. Major Mueller, from Helsingor.

"Well, sir, I had to speak to my supervisor before I picked him up." The way the guard talked, Peter thought he was going to get on his knees or something. Major Mueller was not impressed.

"How many times do I have to tell you that whenever I'm here, *I* am your supervisor?" The major then rattled on too quickly for Peter to catch all the German words, but he could practically feel the heat. The soldier withered in the doorway and backed into Peter's feet.

"Yes, sir," whimpered the guard. "Yes, sir. I understand. Heil Hitler." He saluted with his hand straight out and over his head before he turned around. Then he glared at Peter, as if Peter were to blame for all his troubles. "Get in there, kid," he sneered.

Peter stumbled into the large, wood-paneled office, thinking he would be all alone again with Major Mueller. Instead, he saw Elise sitting in a chair next to the large teak desk, looking nervous. The major swiveled around in his desk chair to face them.

"Please"—he pointed at another chair next to his desk—"sit down."

Then he swiveled back to gaze out of his large window. Beyond was a lake rimmed with bare March trees. On the far end was the Frederiksberg district of Copenhagen, with large blocks of pretty apartment houses. Here and there older buildings and tall church steeples cut into the picture. Peter only glanced out for a moment, then he looked over at his sister to make sure she was okay. She nodded back at him.

"You like my view?" asked Major Mueller. "I'm only here once a week, and my friends here in Copenhagen are kind enough to reserve this beautiful office for me. You like it?" He didn't wait for them to answer but turned back to face them. "During the summer, I've sat here and watched kids like you sail their small boats on the lake there." He paused and put his fingers together. "That's a good thing for children your age to be doing, isn't it?"

Peter knew he couldn't answer this man, even these innocent-sounding questions. He scooted his foot over underneath the edge of the desk to rest it right next to Elise's foot. The major leaned forward at his desk and drilled a hole with his stare. This was the man who could go from syrupy sweet to hard as steel in less than a moment.

"Now you kids listen to me very carefully." He pronounced his Danish words precisely, as if thinking very hard about what he was saying. "I hear that my colleague Colonel Ludheim has been extremely patient with you two, but that so far you have refused this kindness. This is going to change." He reached into his top drawer for something. He pulled out a package of chewing gum and slipped two sticks of the treat across the top of the polished teak desk. "Here, why don't you two have a piece of gum?"

Peter's mouth watered. He hadn't had gum in two years because of the war. *Where did Major Mueller get that kind of thing?* he wondered. He could taste it in his mouth already, but . . .

"No thank you," Elise answered first. She crossed her arms stubbornly and leaned back in her chair. Peter sighed quietly. He wasn't going to take the gum either, he supposed.

"No?" The major shrugged. "I thought all kids liked gum. You Danish kids are different."

He pulled the gum back and squeezed it in his fist. Then he looked up at them again, and Peter could sense the evil glare he had seen before. Peter started to sweat, though the office was cool. Once more, the major leaned forward.

"Let me explain this as plainly as I can so that I am sure you understand." The man pointed at Peter with a crooked finger as he talked. "Up to now you have been treated as honored guests here."

Not quite, thought Peter.

"But you have chosen not to cooperate with us." The major leaned back in his chair, pulled the wrapper off his chewing gum, and popped the treat into his mouth. "Now, I'd like to make you an offer. Normally, we take people like you down into the basement the first day of their visit, and we deal with them. It helps loosen up the conversations." He fixed his black eyes on Peter, then Elise. "Do you understand my meaning?"

Peter understood. The man was talking about some kind of torture. Frank hadn't told him much about it, but Peter knew it was going on.

Major Mueller continued. "Your case has been highly unusual, however," he said, tapping his fingers together. "We haven't taken you two children through the normal steps yet. My instructions to these people here were to give you a good scare. Frankly, I thought it would take a day or two at the most to reach an agreement. It has now been four days since you were first taken into custody."

Peter thought he understood what the major was getting at. Because they were kids, they hadn't gone straight to the rough part. He closed his eyes for a second and saw Frank's bruises. When he opened his eyes again, he looked past the major's shoulder and out the window. Something over the lake caught his attention. A couple of swans were flying low, far across on the other side. Even though it was a gray and dreary March day, Peter would have given almost anything to be out there now.

"Are you listening to me?" The major raised his voice a notch.

"I hear you," replied Peter.

"Well, then hear this." Major Mueller brought his chair back level with a jolt. "I'm telling you that if you don't start cooperating, and cooperating now, we're on our way down to the basement. The pretty girl here is first." Then he grinned his sickly smile at Peter, and Peter had to look away. "You wouldn't want to see your sister get hurt now, would you?"

They were trapped, and all Peter could feel was a rage growing inside him. If they kept quiet, someone was going to hurt Elise. She was the one who had already suffered the most, sitting for hours alone in the little cell. Was there something, maybe a small bit of information, that would satisfy these men? Peter thought about what might happen if he told everything they knew now. What would be the worst that could happen? He was pretty sure that he would not be able to let Elise get hurt . . . but he couldn't think about it anymore.

"Well?" asked the major. "Doesn't it make more sense to you now?" Neither of them moved. "Answer me!" thundered the major, bringing his fist down on the desk.

"I understand what you're saying," Peter whispered. He couldn't keep his hands from shaking, so he hid them under the table. The major reached into his desk again, brought out something in his hand, and slapped it on top of the desk. Peter immediately recognized what it was. The parts from the printing press they had hidden in the fish!

"Now then," the major smiled. "This will help you to remember a little better, won't it? It's a good thing our cook discovered these items before serving the fish to the general." Major Mueller shifted in his chair once more and leaned over to speak into a small box on the corner of the desk. "Heide, would you please bring in the young lady from Helsingor? The one that used to work in my office there?"

The smirk on Major Mueller's face gave Peter even more chills. *Who is he talking about?*

"There's someone I would like you to meet," said Major Mueller, rising to his feet. "Or actually, I believe you've already met, correct?"

The door swung open as Peter and Elise turned to see a woman being led in by another guard. There was something familiar about her, but she was badly bruised on her face, and her eyes were puffy. She wore a dirty blouse and a ripped brown sweater, and her hair was tangled like a bird's nest. She looked as if she had just come through on the losing end of a bad fight in a back alley. Peter still wasn't sure who she was, but he heard his sister gasp.

"Lisbeth!" said Elise, almost under her breath. Peter took another look. It was!

"Yes, I thought you must have met this young woman," crowed Major Mueller, as if he were introducing a circus act. "Come in, come in, Miss von Schreider. Make yourself comfortable with your little friends here. We were just having a nice chat about printing presses."

Lisbeth stumbled in, and Peter thought she would collapse. He gave her a chair and helped her sit down. But Peter's head was spinning, trying to figure out who this Lisbeth really was: friend or traitor? A quick look over at the major showed that the man was enjoying his show. The master of ceremonies spoke up once more.

"Yes, I believe you've met, haven't you? Back in your hometown? A friend of the family?"

Lisbeth only looked down, her eyes rimmed in dark, puffy circles. She said nothing, and Major Mueller went on in his festive voice.

"For months, I've always wondered: How is it that those filthy illegal newspaper printers are always one step ahead of me? Why does the Underground always seem to know what we're going to do in Helsingor just before it happens?" He got up from his chair, stepped around his desk, and walked over to where Lisbeth sat. Then he bent down and took her chin in his hand.

"Didn't you ever wonder the same thing, Miss von Schrei-der?" He let her chin drop, and she would not look at him.

"You worked in my office for several months ... no ... over a year, correct?"

Lisbeth only nodded weakly.

"Well, as I mentioned, it always bothered me that those criminals could continue to operate, month after month, issue after issue, all the time printing those lies about the Fatherland. It grieved me to see how the ignorant people of Denmark could be so misled by this garbage." He picked up a piece of paper and waved it in front of Peter and Elise. Peter recognized a copy of their own newspaper, *The Free Dane*.

"This garbage," the major repeated. "But every time I thought we had someone cornered, they would slip out of my fingers. One step ahead. It seemed to be a security leak. How did they always find out just in time? How?"

Major Mueller was pacing around the room, making his speech. He hit the palm of one hand with his fist for emphasis.

"Well, I finally found out the other day," continued the major. "And I can tell you, it was a terrible thing to learn." He laughed a long, evil-sounding laugh and stepped over to a table with a metal box the size of a suitcase on it. On the side of the box was a large dial, along with several switches and lights. In gold script was the word "Telegraphone," and on top were two spools of pi-ano wire strung together. Peter thought he knew what it was, but he wasn't sure.

"Have you ever heard a wire recorder before?" Major Mueller asked Peter. Peter shook his head.

"We have here an invention to store the human voice," explained the major, looking proud of his machine. "A Danish invention, by the way, though of course our German technology has greatly improved on the concept. So would you like to turn the switch?" The major smiled his dark smile, and again Peter shook his head no. Peter didn't care who had invented this thing; he knew he didn't want to touch it.

"Turn the switch!" roared the major. He grabbed the back of Peter's neck and pulled him to his feet by his shirt collar. Coughing, Peter stood and reached for the switch on the wire recorder.

"That's my boy," crooned the major. "That switch on the left. Just turn it to the left."

Peter had never had his hands on this kind of a machine before, and he wasn't quite sure what it was going to do. But he did as Major Mueller instructed, and the spools started turning. There was a scratchy noise, and then a voice—a faint voice, but Peter could tell plainly whose it was.

"Sounds just like her, doesn't it?" asked Major Mueller. "Miss von Schreider sounds quite good on the recording. My technician figured out a way to record our telephone conversations for security purposes, and this is the kind of thing I learned. Enlightening, wouldn't you say?"

Peter and Elise strained to understand what Lisbeth was saying on the recording, and they leaned forward.

"Please put me through to Bella three-seven-six-six," said Lisbeth's voice on the recording. "And hurry."

Lisbeth didn't look up from her chair. A moment later Peter heard the unmistakably clear voice of his mother answer the phone, then Lisbeth introduced herself.

"There's no time," said the voice. "I think this line is safe, but I'm not sure. Your children are being held here at Nazi Command Headquarters on King Street. I think they're in trouble."

"Who is this?" asked the voice of Peter and Elise's mother. Peter had to remind himself that this was just some kind of machine, not his mother's real voice.

"Just a friend," said Lisbeth's voice. "Hurry, I believe they're in trouble, mixed up with something."

Major Mueller clicked off his machine and smiled. The two doughnut-sized spools on top stopped spinning. "There's more. But it's pretty amazing, wouldn't you say? Someday everyone is going to have one of these, but today, it's only for German Army Intelligence." He shoved Peter back down in his chair and whirled to face Lisbeth once more. He pointed a bony finger in her face, but she pretended not to notice.

"It's fortunate that we can confirm everything you said, Miss von Schreider—every filthy word you uttered to the enemies of the Reich. Calls to Resistance workers as well, passing along important information. Would you like to hear more? It's down on the wire, and it's been recorded on paper and filed in the proper place. Yes!" He clapped his hands and smiled. "We finally figured out who it was who was calling the Danish criminals, who was warning them of our activities, who was trying to fight against us even as she pretended to work for us. So you see, Miss von Schreider, you will regret this treachery most deeply. I promise you will regret it for the rest of your short life. Your *very* short life." He chuckled once more.

Peter trembled even more than before. This was not a game. Major Mueller was serious. Deadly serious. Was there a reason he and Elise were being made to stay here and listen to this?

"So, my two young friends," said Major Mueller as he circled around once more to sit down behind the desk. "You may be wondering why you're sitting here. Why am I making you listen to this depressing story? It's very simple.

"Your friend Miss von Schreider has gotten herself into a fine mess, I'd say. Quite serious, as you understand." He looked straight at Elise, and she looked away.

"Look at me, young lady!" he shouted. "I want you to understand what I'm saying."

Elise slowly raised her glance, and Peter could feel her pain. More than that, he wanted to jump up and push the man out of his chair.

"We usually shoot these kind of traitors without further delay." Major Mueller drummed his fingers against the desk. "However, what I'm telling you is that we may be able to strike a bargain."

"Leave these children out of this," objected Lisbeth, raising her head. "They have nothing to do with this."

Major Mueller looked surprised, but a smile played at the corner of his mouth.

"Oh, so now she comes to life, does she?" he mocked Lisbeth. "Well, just let me explain my proposition to our mutual friend here, so that she and her brother can decide for themselves."

Lisbeth's eyes glimmered with tears, and she looked down once more. The major turned to Elise.

"Now, young lady, as I was saying, I have a proposition to make for you and your brother. You appear to be the intelligent one of the group, and I should think you will understand the seriousness of your friend's situation. You understand this?"

Elise nodded but avoided Major Mueller's dark eyes.

"And you also understand that your friend has only a short time to live?"

"Oh, come now, Major," Lisbeth objected again, this time in German. "You can make your deals with me."

"I will thank you to shut up, my dear Miss von Schreider." The major didn't look at Lisbeth as he spoke. "You have nothing to deal with, I'm afraid. Nothing to offer. But the children do, you see? They still have some information they can trade. Perhaps even for your life. Now do you understand? A straight trade." He turned to Peter. "You tell us where the illegal newspaper is, and I'll consider sparing your friend here. What a bargain."

The major leaned back in his chair and surveyed the three of them. "Need time to discuss the deal?" He sounded like a salesman in a department store. "By all means. Figure out the best thing to do." Then he looked at his wristwatch and stifled a yawn. "I'll give you a minute to discuss this. No one could ever complain that I haven't been generous." He put his feet up on the desk, leaned back in his chair, and closed his eyes.

For a moment, Peter couldn't move but stared out the window past Major Mueller. Out on the lake the swans were flying again, and then three other flying specks caught his eye.

The flat specks flew over Frederiksberg's red rooftops, wheeled around in formation, and headed straight for their building. In an instant, Peter knew these were no swans. Another speck joined the three, and for a moment, there was no doubt about the shape of the planes. Peter had a picture of one back home on his bedroom wall, next to his bed. The planes had to be—yes, he was positive.

They were British Spitfire fighters.

Peter's first impulse was to shout out a warning, but he instantly thought better of that. Instead, he leaned over and pulled Elise around to where Lisbeth was sitting, keeping an eye on Major Mueller.

"Don't say a word," he mouthed to Elise and Lisbeth, praying at the same time that the other two would understand him and that Major Mueller would keep his eyes closed.

Peter pointed out the window at the approaching planes and mouthed, "British bombers."

Elise and Lisbeth nodded, and Peter glanced up nervously to see how much time they had. The specks were getting much larger, and Peter's heart raced along with them. In a moment, the major would probably hear the roar from their engines, but then it would be too late. He was still leaning back in his chair with his eyes closed, with no idea that his world would come crashing around his head in just—

"Just about ten seconds." Peter was whispering now. "At the count of three, grab the edge of the desk and help me dump it." Peter could barely get the words out. Elise nodded.

"I think that's a good plan," said Lisbeth, loud enough for everyone in the room to hear. She moved her hands over to the edge of the desk with Peter's and Elise's. Major Mueller smiled and straightened up in his chair.

"Yes?" He looked like someone who had just won a game of checkers. But Peter only focused on the line of planes, now roaring straight for the window. Peter saw the first plane pull up and release two bombs. It looked as if the British pilot was aiming for the basement.

"Now!" shouted Peter, forgetting to count. The first planes looked as if they were going to fly in the window, but at the last minute they wheeled around out of sight. Still, there was no explosion.

Peter, Elise, and Lisbeth all stood up and grabbed the edge of the desk, heaving with all their strength. They dumped it over on the astonished Major Mueller's lap, and he slid over backward in his chair, sputtering.

"You little fools!" he bellowed. "Guards!"

INTO THE FLAMES

The twins didn't stay around to hear the rest of Major Mueller's yells. They both scrambled for the door, leaving him with the desk in his lap. Lisbeth was right behind them. They dashed toward the stairway, with guards shouting behind them. No one looked back.

They hadn't even reached the stairs when the first explosion rocked the building. As if they were in some mighty earthquake, they fell to their knees while windows shattered around them. Peter covered his head and felt tiny shards of glass shower all over him. A second later, he looked up to see Lisbeth and Elise covered with plaster that was flaking from the walls and ceiling. They got to their feet and shook off like dogs.

"Through here!" he yelled. "We've got to go up and see if we can do something upstairs."

"Where?" asked Lisbeth, wiping the dust out of her eyes.

"Upstairs!" shouted Elise. There was another explosion from somewhere below them, and they ducked more flying plaster.

"Up in the attic," explained Peter. "All the Resistance people are locked up. Maybe we can—"

The next series of blasts, deep rumbles from within the building, drowned out his voice. But Peter had already said enough for Lisbeth to understand.

"You lead the way," said Lisbeth, heading for the stairway.

The stairway was even worse than the hallway. With each blast, more of the walls would shake, teeter, and fall. Twice, they had to stop and hold on to the railings while the entire stairway shook from the impact of the bombs. None of the Germans rushing down noticed them, and Peter tried not to look at anyone. Many were hurt; two soldiers were helping a third, practically dragging him down the stairs. Everywhere there was dust, falling walls, and shouting.

Finally they made it up the last stairway to the attic and stepped out into more wreckage. Somewhere outside, an air-raid siren finally went off, and gunfire made a peppering, popping sound. Peter didn't know if it was the Germans or the British planes doing the shooting. Maybe both.

"Left," said Peter, pulling Elise by the arm. But the hallway looked different now than when he had come this way earlier with the major.

"No, Peter, it's this way!" Elise tugged back, and for a moment Peter froze. Lisbeth bumped into them from behind. Another explosion rocked the building, and part of the hallway ahead of them crashed into splinters. He felt the floor lean toward the latest explosion. Someone up ahead was coming out of the cloud of smoke and dust, and Peter recognized an older guard who had opened their cells for meals.

"Hey!" shouted Peter above the crackle of gunfire outside. It was coming louder now, and there was more of it. "Mr. Guard!"

The man staggered closer, holding his head. There was blood on the man's hand, and he seemed not to notice them.

"The keys," pleaded Elise when he stopped.

Peter stepped up to the man, who was leaning over, teetering. "Give us the keys so we can get these prisoners out of here, at least down to the bomb shelter."

"No." The man's voice sounded far away, hoarse. "It's too late. Too late for all of us. We're all going to die." He straightened up, then brushed the dust off his uniform with his free hand. He looked past Peter's shoulder down the hall and started mumbling.

"You don't understand!" said Peter. "It's not too late. We just have to have the keys. Give us the keys." He felt as if he were talking to a deaf person, and Peter wasn't quite sure if the guard was on the same planet anymore.

"Oh, the keys," the man said, still looking down the hall. "The keys." He reached into his jacket pocket, fished around for a moment, and then pulled out a pair of scissors, dangling them out in front of himself. He teetered once more.

"Come on, Elise," said Peter, giving up on the man. He went up behind the German and quickly reached into jacket pockets, then shirt pockets, then pants pockets. The man didn't move, only stood there, staring down the hall, mumbling. Finally, Peter's hand closed around a cluster of keys.

"Got them!" said Peter just as a blast peeled the ceiling away. Elise and Lisbeth ducked in time, but when Peter stepped out and away, he was met by a falling beam. It glanced off his shoulder but swept him off his feet. He landed on his back next to the dazed German, who still hadn't moved.

"Ooh, what hit me?" Peter wasn't sure if he could get up. The beam, with a considerable piece of ceiling and a bunch of wiring, had parked itself next to his head. For a moment, all he could hear was Elise screaming in his ear.

"Are you all right, Peter? Are you all right?"

He groaned out a reply, but it hurt to move his lips. "Just get this stuff off me."

Peter heard more screaming as Elise and Lisbeth clawed at the rubble to get him out. He thought he heard other shouts too, from behind doors. There was a crash just above where Peter was lying as another piece of the ceiling fell.

"Wake up!" Elise was shouting. "You've got to help me get my brother out of there!"

A minute later Peter was looking into his sister's face, or at least someone who looked like his sister. He was still a bit dazed.

"Are you okay?" Elise pulled another piece of plaster off his leg, and Peter wiggled free. He looked up to see the guard shuffling slowly down the hall again, still mumbling.

Elise helped Peter get up. "Are you sure you're okay?"

Peter wiggled his body gently, and everything seemed to work. There was a long gash on his left arm, though, where a nail had caught him and ripped through the sleeve on his shirt.

"Feels like somebody punched me real good in the face," he said, trying to act more brave than he felt. "But I'm okay." Then he remembered why they had come up there. "But the keys!"

"The keys," echoed Elise, and she started clawing through the pile of rubble. She looked over at him for a second and stopped. "You're still holding them!"

Peter looked down at his fist. Somehow, he hadn't let go.

"How about that?" He jingled the ring and shook his head. Then another piece of ceiling caved in. Lisbeth looked around in the ruins.

"Do you smell smoke?" she asked.

Peter whiffed the air, and it hurt to move his nose. He couldn't tell, with all the dust and things flying around in the air.

"I don't smell a thing," he said. He turned to the first door in the hallway of prison cells and started trying keys. The first and the second keys didn't fit. The third key went in but wouldn't turn.

"I'm sure of it," said Lisbeth. "There's a fire underneath us now. Can't you smell it?"

Elise put her head down to the floor, then came up again. "I think I smell it," she said, sniffing once more.

"Well, then I need to get this stupid key working, don't I?" Peter was sweating now and shaking.

"Come on," urged Elise, hopping up and down. "How many keys can there be?"

"I'm going as fast as I can," Peter yelled back, trying the seventh key backward and forward. *Please, Lord,* he pleaded in a silent prayer. *Help!* A moment later something clicked.

"It worked!" he cried. "This one worked!"

Elise stood beside him and yanked the door open, then pulled back in horror. Peter saw it too: Half of the floor of the small cell was blown away, and timbers pointed every which way like broken toothpicks. Outside British planes were screaming in and out of clouds of smoke, and gunfire peppered the morning air. Back in the building, only a small piece of what had been the floor was left. Someone was balancing on that ledge, trying not to fall five stories down.

"Over here!" yelled the prisoner. He looked more like a scarecrow than a man. His clothes were ripped, but he was alive. "Keep the door open. I'm coming right over."

The man gingerly stepped across a beam to come up close to the open door. There was still a gap, though, and Peter was afraid to look down. The man couldn't reach the safety of the door.

"Here," said Lisbeth, pushing through. "We've got to make some sort of chain." She looked around for something with which to reach out to the man, but there was nothing. Another plane screamed by, close enough for Peter to see a pilot inside the cockpit.

"Here, I've got it," said Peter, unbuckling his belt. "Lisbeth, you lean out, and I'll hold you with my belt. Elise can hold on to me. Then you can grab the guy when he jumps."

Lisbeth looked around once more, then down at the four-foot gap that separated the prisoner from safety. She nodded, and Peter handed her the end of his looped belt.

"Okay," Lisbeth shouted to the man, who seemed to be holding on with his fingernails. "I'm going to lean out, and you have to jump for our ledge. We'll hold on to you, okay?"

The man looked frightened but nodded. Lisbeth leaned out

and held out her free hand. The man coiled up, then sprang and pulled on Lisbeth's arm. The next minute, they all tumbled back into the hallway.

"I don't know where you all came from," said the man, getting to his feet. "But you must be some kind of angels."

Peter took the keys out of his pocket and turned toward another of the unopened doors.

"No!" shouted the man, grabbing Peter's arm. "This building is going to collapse!"

Peter yanked his arm away from the thin man in disgust. "We're not leaving until we get the rest of these doors open. You leave if you want to."

Elise was tugging at one door that looked as if its hinges were loose. "Come on, Peter! There's no time!"

The scarecrow man finally moved, as if he had changed his mind about running.

"Here, give me the keys," he said. "I'll help you."

"Never mind," replied Peter, heading for the door where Elise was. "I've got it."

The next few doors went easier; Peter would unlock the door, then run to the one beside it. Elise, Lisbeth, and the scarecrow man pulled open the doors and helped prisoners who were inside get down the hall to the stairwell. But now Peter could smell the smoke, and he wasn't at all sure if they could make it out of the building. Two more bombs exploded in the courtyard, and sirens started wailing from somewhere in the city. This had to be a dream, Peter decided. A very, very bad dream.

"Only a few more doors," urged Elise. They were almost to their own cells. Elise's would be empty, Peter knew, but his Bible-reading friend and Tiger would still be locked up. He reached for the next-to-last door, turned the key, and yanked it open. Frank Nielsen was standing there with the cat in his arms. Peter wasn't sure whose eyes were wider. Without a word, Frank handed over the cat.

"Are you all right, Frank?" asked Peter.

Frank shook his head, as if he were dreaming. "Never better," he whispered. Then he jumped out of the room, but paused for a moment as he passed Peter. He tucked his little black Bible into Peter's pants pocket. "Take this too."

There wasn't time to say anything; Peter just nodded and followed Frank as they were rocked by another blast. Then Peter headed for the last door. He looked over his shoulder, down the now-empty hall. "But what happened to the scarecrow man?"

"That skinny fellow?" asked Frank. "He's one of the ringers I was telling you about. He works for the Germans."

Peter paused for a second and thought of Lisbeth leaning out over the bombed-out building trying to save the man.

"Doesn't matter," said Lisbeth quietly. "He needed help."

Frank looked up and down the halls. "Well, he's gone now."

Elise rattled the doorknob across the hall from Peter's old cell. She had taken the squirming and meowing Tiger under her arm. "Last door, Peter," she urged him on.

"I'm coming," replied Peter. "But what about that other room?" He pointed to an open door across the hall.

"My old room, remember?" replied Elise. "Nothing there—"

As she ran by, Elise reached into her room, grabbed a pile of papers, and stuffed them into the front pocket of her pants. Peter didn't have time to ask her what they were.

"Let's check this last room and get out of here," Frank yelled.

The last cell was separated from the others by a small storage area, and inside the room it was dark and shadowy. Half of the ceiling had fallen in.

"Must have been empty," declared Frank, giving one of the boards a kick.

They were just about to turn and go when another blast hit the building and part of the ceiling crumbled on top of them. Everyone ducked, and Tiger squirted out of Elise's grasp.

"Tiger!" Peter yelled. "You come back here!"

"Don't run in under there, kitty," called Elise as she followed the cat under a pile of boards that had fallen next to the room's bunk. She fell to her knees and started digging at the hole where the cat had disappeared.

"Let him go!" screamed Frank. "There's no time to be hunting for a cat."

"But we can't just leave him here," protested Peter, joining his sister.

Frank yanked at Peter's shirt. "Listen, kids, we—"

He stopped short at the sound of a groan from somewhere under the pile of boards, then he let go of Peter's shirt and threw himself down on the floor to listen. Lisbeth rushed in from the hall and kneeled down too.

"Did you hear that?" asked Elise. She stopped pulling boards from the pile to listen. For a moment, everything outside was still. Now the building itself seemed to be groaning and swaying, as if it were losing a prizefight.

"I heard it," croaked Peter. "And it sure wasn't Tiger."

Frank desperately started pulling off boards and plaster. "I heard it too. Let's get this junk off."

Everyone worked frantically, pulling off the largest boards first. Lisbeth coughed at the dust, then a moment later let out a frightened yelp.

"I just felt something." She was gasping, trying to breathe in the dust fog. "Someone's hand, I think."

Everyone joined Lisbeth where she had been digging, pulling off debris almost in a frenzy.

"I felt something too," cried Peter. "Feels like a shirt. Frank, remember what I asked you about my uncle?"

"I remember," replied Frank, wiping his brow with the back of his gritty hand. "But with that closet in the hall, this room was cut off from the others."

Peter thought about the voices he had heard during the night, the voices that seemed like a dream. Had the guards really said "Andersen"? The body under the rubble groaned again and tried to roll over. Elise pushed one more board out of the way to reveal a man's leg.

"There he is," Frank coughed. "I think we can get him out now."

The man under the rubble coughed, and shook, and coughed again.

"Hey," came a man's weak voice. "Is somebody out there?"

"Hold still," yelled Frank. "We almost have you out of there."

"I'm right here," came the voice once more.

Lisbeth stopped her digging for a moment and stared at the pile of plaster where the voice was coming from. "Morten?" she asked, her voice trembling. "Morten?"

The small mountain of rubbish started to tremble. As Peter and Elise wildly pulled off a large beam, they could tell that the body was trying to get up. Peter had known who it was with the man's first word. He had just been afraid to say what Lisbeth had just said.

"Hold still down there," warned Frank. "You're going to hurt yourself more than you already are."

But it was too late. With a heave, Peter, Elise, and Lisbeth pried loose the last beam, and the man from underneath the pile sat up in an eruption of plaster and dust. Lisbeth practically dove to the floor to embrace the ghostly-looking figure, but she only narrowly beat Peter and Elise.

"I knew it was you!" Peter cried, burying his face in Uncle Morten's shoulder. Elise and Lisbeth had their arms around his neck and Morten was laughing.

Frank sputtered a protest. "How about letting this man get up before you attack him!"

Peter stood back for a moment, while Elise and Lisbeth helped Uncle Morten up from both sides. He teetered, put his hand to his forehead, and then stood firm. His beard looked as if it had been powdered with makeup, and all Peter could see of his face was a wide, toothy grin.

Uncle Morten looked around at his rescuers with a look of amazement. "I certainly don't know what's going on here, friends. But we should move now and talk later." He looked down at Peter and Elise. "You look like my niece and nephew, but I think you're angels. We *are* alive, aren't we?"

"For now," interrupted Frank. "But we won't be if we keep standing around chatting."

"Right," agreed Morten. He shook his arms and legs as he headed for the door. He paused a moment, looking both ways down the hall at the wreckage.

"I think I can find the way out," volunteered Peter.

"Well, then, Peter, why don't you and your friend—"

"Frank Nielsen," Peter put in.

"Okay, why don't you and Frank lead the way? We'll follow you until we get to the ground floor."

As Peter started down the hall, a flash of fur streaked by. He had forgotten about the cat. "Tiger!" he yelled. "There you are."

Tiger sat down at the end of the hallway and looked back at the group as if he had been waiting for hours. He licked a paw nervously.

Without slowing down, Frank reached down, picked up the animal by the back of the neck, and handed him to Peter. "Don't let him get in the way."

Peter held Tiger under his arm as they hurried down the hallway, and another series of blasts hit the building. The floor quivered like sponge cake, and Peter was sure it would open up and drop them five stories. There was no mistaking the smoke now. Peter's eyes burned and watered. The cat under his arm meowed in confusion.

"It's okay, Tiger." He stroked the cat's head. "We'll get you out of here in just a minute."

As he spoke, another section of ceiling came crashing in. Everyone ducked, and the ceiling covered them with another layer of dust. They were all gagging and coughing as they threaded their way through the maze of fallen walls, broken glass, and hanging wires. When they reached the stairway, Uncle Morten grabbed Peter's shoulder.

"We need a plan," said Uncle Morten, taking charge. There

was a chatter of machine gun fire outside, and Peter heard another plane buzzing overhead.

"Let's everybody stick close together," put in Frank, looking around nervously.

"All right, then," decided Uncle Morten, nodding at Peter and Frank. "I'll lead the way from here."

As he followed his uncle down the shadowy stairway, Peter thought of the verse Frank had read to the person in the cell next to them. *When you walk through the fire, you will not be burned; the flames will not set you ablaze.* The only difference now was that they were going to run through the fire, not walk.

Peter knew he had to do something about Tiger while he still had a chance. With his free hand he unbuttoned the top button of his shirt and stuffed the animal inside.

"Ride in there, Tiger," Peter whispered. Somehow, the kitten seemed to understand—and didn't try to climb out.

Uncle Morten led the way down, followed by Lisbeth, Elise, Peter with his cat, and finally Frank. Every few feet, they had to stoop under fallen walls and sidestep hanging boards and beams. In the darkest sections, Peter held on to Elise's hand in front of him. Once Tiger peeked out from inside Peter's shirt but made no sound.

"Almost there," Uncle Morten called back over his shoulder. They had still not come across any more soldiers—none who were alive anyway. Peter closed his eyes several times, trying to stay in control of his stomach. He had never seen the war this close up. Elise held firmly to his hand, and everyone was coughing.

When they reached the ground floor, they stopped before opening the door. Heavy black smoke curled under the bottom of the door. It smelled like dirty fireworks, and it made everyone choke even worse. Peter tried to wipe the sting out of his eyes on his shirt-sleeve.

"If we run into anyone," commanded Uncle Morten, his hand on the doorknob, "everyone run ahead and I'll deal with it."

Peter started to protest. "We can't just leave—"

"This isn't a vote." Uncle Morten cut him off sharply. "Got it?"

Everyone froze as more guns popped outside. Peter nodded, then followed his uncle through the door, which fell off its hinges as they shoved it open. It was the same office he had been through once before, the first night they had been brought to this place. But now flames had taken over the rubble in wild bonfires all over the destroyed room. Peter couldn't even make out a hallway.

"Ow!" cried Lisbeth from somewhere behind them. Peter looked over his shoulder to see her sprawled facedown on the floor. She struggled quickly to her knees and looked up. Pain was written all over her face, and she rocked back and forth as she held her foot.

"Stupid," muttered Lisbeth as the others ran back to her. "I'm so stupid. My foot caught under that board." She pointed to a protruding piece of wood.

"Can you walk on it?" asked Uncle Morten, concern breaking through his voice. He helped her to her feet and tried to let go, but she almost fell. Tears made tracks down her dirty, swollen cheeks.

"I'm so sorry," she cried. "I can't even walk. I—"

"Doesn't matter," interrupted Uncle Morten. "Hold on."

In one sweeping motion Uncle Morten had Lisbeth in his arms, and he continued picking his way across the rubble of the bombed-out first floor through the smoke.

All Peter could see was black smoke, most of it billowing up from gaping holes in the floor. Putting his arm in front of his face did no good. He was still coughing, and sweat dripped down his forehead as flames licked up at them. It was all he could do to keep up with Elise.

Somehow everyone made it across the room without falling into any of the fire holes. Outside, the air-raid sirens were still screaming. Uncle Morten put Lisbeth down for a moment in the courtyard in front of the building, and the five of them crouched by the fragments of a wall, looking for a chance to run. For the first time in days, Peter gulped in cool, fresh air.

In front of them trucks had been tossed around like toys; now they were burning and upside down. Three large craters marked the courtyard. Peter didn't want to look, but he knew in a moment that dozens of guards lay outside on the pavement. The place where the Germans had parked all their cars, across the street, was a rubble heap. At least for the moment, the way was clear.

"Straight through there, Frank?" Uncle Morten pointed at a way through the maze of rubble. Frank nodded.

Without wasting any more time, they followed their uncle again as he half walked, half jogged through the courtyard with Lisbeth in his arms, dodging burning trucks and bomb craters. Peter didn't dare slow down now that they were out in the open. Tiger bounced inside his shirt. Another plane screamed overhead, and they ducked.

Lord, please show us the way out of here, Peter prayed silently. *Show us the way home.* He looked over at Elise, who was running beside him, and her lips were moving too.

"Peter!" Frank's voice behind him was urgent, and Peter stopped for a moment to hide behind a smoldering truck at the edge of the courtyard. Frank came right up next to him and held on to his shoulder.

"This is where I leave you." Frank was looking down a side street. Peter guessed he might disappear into a store or a building.

From somewhere behind them came the sound of machine gun fire. Elise came out from behind the truck next to them, just a couple of feet away.

"Come on, Peter," she called to him. "It's clear."

"She's right," agreed Frank. "Now go. Be sure to read that Bible I gave you." Before Peter had time to think, Frank slapped him on the back and sprinted off in the opposite direction.

"Thanks, Frank," mumbled Peter, tears in his eyes.

"It's clear, Peter!" Elise repeated.

Peter blinked his eyes to keep them from stinging, checked on
Tiger, and followed his sister. They ran to catch up to Uncle Morten and Lisbeth, who had stopped by another smoldering truck
in an area that had once been used as a parking lot. A parade of
screaming ambulances and army trucks was coming into sight
from the direction Frank had run. Other army cars and trucks had
already pulled up to the burning building from another direction.

Just ahead of them and beyond all the burning trucks they
were running through, Peter saw a fence. Beyond them railroad
tracks led to a tunnel. Uncle Morten stopped in front of the wire-
link fence, leaned Lisbeth against it, and turned around. He bent
over, made a stirrup with his hands, and nodded to Elise. Instantly she stepped up and nearly flew over the fence. Peter followed, trying not to squish Tiger. Once they were on the other
side the twins helped Lisbeth struggle over.

Lisbeth tried to take a step once she was over, but she only
crumpled to her knees in the gravel next to four sets of railroad
tracks. Peter attempted to pull her up, while Uncle Morten scaled
the fence and hopped down to their side.

"You already showed us that you can't walk," Uncle Morten
reminded her. He picked her up again and turned toward the
dark mouth of the tunnel. Peter figured it was twenty, maybe
thirty steps away.

"Where does this lead to, Uncle?" asked Peter as they started
jogging once more. "Do you know where we're going?"

Uncle Morten didn't get a chance to answer. A shrill whistle
blew from somewhere behind them, from the other side of the
fence.

"You there!" came a sharp German voice. "Halt right where
you are."

THE TUNNEL

No one turned around. Uncle Morten ran as fast as he could with Lisbeth still in his arms. The shouting continued behind them, and then Peter heard the popping of gunfire. Gravel sprayed an arm's length to his left and hit him on the cheek.

"Inside!" commanded Uncle Morten, but no one needed an invitation to dive into the shadows of the railroad tunnel. It smelled of mold and the exhaust smoke of trains, but it was dark and away from the man with the gun. Peter shivered and kept running with one hand on Tiger. Somehow the kitten was still hanging on inside his shirt.

"Where is everyone?" asked Peter in a loud whisper. His eyes were still getting used to the blackness. His voice echoed.

"We're all here," answered Uncle Morten. "Elise?"

"Yeah," came Elise's quivering voice. She was right next to Peter but seemed very small and far away.

"Okay," said Uncle Morten. "We can't stop now."

They started jogging through the tunnel, trying not to trip over the rails.

Peter tried to keep track of his sister, but all he could do was listen for her breathing. In the darkness, the sound got louder and louder, until Elise was rasping and coughing. Peter thought he probably didn't sound much better. In a few minutes, her coughing turned to sobbing.

"Elise, are you okay?" Peter asked for the tenth time.

But Elise didn't answer. By then she was crying loudly, and Peter groped in the darkness to see where she was. His hand brushed up against a wall, and it was damp and gritty.

"I can't!" cried Elise. "I just can't . . . run . . . anymore. I'm too . . ."

In the shadows Peter saw his sister stop to rest, with her hands on her knees.

"Yes you can." Lisbeth hopped over to Elise and leaned on her shoulder. Her voice was urgent but gentle. "I'm the only one who can't run anymore. Let's help each other."

"Shh!" whispered Uncle Morten. "There's still someone back there. Keep going!"

"Let's go," urged Lisbeth.

Elise choked back another sob, and let Lisbeth lean on her as Uncle Morten ran ahead to lead the way. Together they hobbled after Uncle Morten like runners in a three-legged race. But this was no picnic, Peter thought as they hurried deeper into the curving tunnel.

By then, Peter was shaking all over, and not because he was cold. He wasn't sure how much longer Tiger would let himself be packed around inside his shirt. He wished he could sit down and cry too.

A minute later, the whistle followed them inside. They heard it echo all around them until Peter couldn't tell if the sounds were coming from behind or ahead. Elise and Lisbeth stumbled once in the oily gravel but didn't fall all the way.

"Just a little farther," urged Uncle Morten. "I think we're way ahead of them."

Peter was glad his uncle sounded so sure; it seemed to Peter as if the man with the whistle was only a few steps back, the way the shrill noise rang in their ears. At one point, the tracks split into a "Y," and Uncle Morten led them to the right, sometimes jogging ahead to see where the tunnel went. Finally, Peter saw a dull, gray light up ahead.

When they came out on the other side, they were in the heart of the city, near the main railroad station. With Uncle Morten's help, Peter and Elise vaulted over another six-foot fence, then turned to help Lisbeth once more. Peter's side ached, and he expected a squad of German soldiers to come charging out of the mouth of the tunnel at any moment.

"Come on, Lisbeth," urged Elise, trying to get her breath. "We'll catch you." It was her turn to be the encourager.

Uncle Morten hoisted Lisbeth up on the other side, and for a moment she winced with pain as she caught her leg on something sharp.

"Watch out for the edge of that thing," warned Uncle Morten too late. "It's wicked."

Lisbeth fell the rest of the way, but the twins caught her in time. Once Uncle Morten made it over, he and Peter supported Lisbeth on both sides. Together they scrambled down a gravel slope and made their way into a downtown neighborhood of streets, shops, and tall old buildings. Most people hurried along with their collars pulled up against the chill, ignoring them. Peter couldn't help looking behind him, but he saw no one come out of the tunnel.

"Here, give me the cat, Peter," offered Elise. "I'm okay now."

Peter sighed in relief and let his sister fish the kitten out of his shirt.

They tried to look as normal as possible, with Lisbeth leaning heavily on Uncle Morten and trying not to limp. But their clothes were dirty and ripped, and Peter prayed they wouldn't run into any more German soldiers before they got to wherever they were going. Uncle Morten was still hurrying them along.

"Where are we going, Uncle?" Elise asked first.

Uncle Morten said nothing, just looked over at Lisbeth. She

answered for him. "My parents' home. They live here in the city."

Peter raised his eyebrows. He could still imagine the men in the tunnel, somewhere behind them. "Do the Germans know where they live?" he asked.

Lisbeth shook her head. "I've never told anyone. As far as Major Mueller is concerned, I'm an orphan. We'll just warm up, clean up, and leave again."

Peter caught the scent of freshly baked bread and looked for the bakery they must have passed. He took a deep breath to try to eat the wonderful smell.

"I smell it too," whispered Uncle Morten. He had been in prison a lot longer than anyone.

The street they were on reminded Peter of their home, only the gray stone buildings seemed taller, the streets a little wider. Somewhere close by was the big Tivoli Gardens Amusement Park—still closed for the winter—and the Central Square. Peter and Elise had been there a few times before. Happier times.

The sidewalks were filled with people on black bicycles, just like back home in Helsingor. As they hurried along, no one seemed to give them a second look, except for an older man in a small hardware store who stared curiously out his window at them. The man nodded his head and disappeared back into his shop.

Peter couldn't relax yet. He shivered in the cold and looked up at the high, gray clouds. It would have been nice to have his heavy coat, the one he left behind somewhere in the fire. And every block or two, he looked nervously back over his shoulder. Once he thought he saw a familiar figure about a half block behind them. If they weren't holding on to Lisbeth, Peter would have run as fast as he could.

"Elise," he said to his sister, his voice cracking. "Look behind us, but don't look like you're looking." Elise glanced back over her shoulder at the crowd. "Do you see someone following us? I think it's that guy from the bombed-out room. Mr. Scarecrow, you know? See him, back there next to that trolley?"

"I don't see a thing, except for a lot of people, Peter. Why would he be following us? Just relax."

Uncle Morten looked back too and quickly scanned the crowd. "I don't see anyone," he agreed. "But let's go a little faster. This is Westbridge Street. We're almost there. Turn left." They picked up their pace, while Peter kept looking back over his shoulder. He didn't see the man he thought he saw before. *Maybe I'm just imagining things,* he told himself.

Westbridge Street was wider than the smaller avenue they had been on, full of traffic, but again mostly bicycles. This street had small, bare trees every few feet in neat little holes in the sidewalk. A few trucks and buses threaded their way through the early afternoon crowd. And in the distance about a block ahead of them, Peter could see a German truck parting the crowds, coming their direction.

A uniformed man was standing up in the back of the open end of the truck, bundled up against the chill. He appeared to be searching the crowds for something, or someone. On his right and left, uniformed soldiers with rifles kept watch as well. As the driver laid on his horn, bike riders swerved away in front of the truck. Peter pulled back.

"Uncle Morten—" he said.

"I see them," replied Uncle Morten. "We're almost there."

WATCHER FROM
THE SHADOWS

After glancing up to read the number outside, Uncle Morten pushed everyone through an unlocked door into the small lobby of an apartment building. Peter stumbled inside, where it was quiet, cold, and dim. The older marble floors glowed under a polished brass wall lamp. He buried his face in the paneled wall and tried to catch his breath. Even the faint ammonia smell of the freshly washed flooring seemed welcoming and safe.

"They're out looking for people who got away from the Shell House," suggested Elise, peeking out the apartment building door. Tiger wiggled in her arms, but she held him fast.

"Could be," agreed Uncle Morten, running his finger down a list of names behind a glass case inside the lobby. He squinted in the half-light. "Tell me if they come closer. Let's see, Rydeng, Torp, von . . . here it is."

"Ernst and Brigitta von Schreider. Apartment two fifty-five. Don't you remember, Morten?" asked Lisbeth.

"I've only been here a couple of times," he defended himself.

"The soldiers are about five doors down now," reported Elise.

"This way." Uncle Morten started up a narrow stairway, pulling Lisbeth up with him one step at a time. "You stay off that ankle now. We'll have to get you to a doctor when we get to Sweden—"

"It's fine," she tried to sound brave. "Really. Just a sprain."

"Hmm." Uncle Morten paused at the first landing, and no one said anything else as they struggled up the rest of the stairs.

As they climbed, Peter listened for the sound of the door somewhere downstairs. But there was no sound, no soldiers coming inside, only Lisbeth struggling up each step and Uncle Morten grunting as he tried to lift her up. Halfway up Peter heard a baby squealing from behind someone's door. Someone else coughed.

"Just up here to the right," said Lisbeth. As they came to the top of the first stairway she pointed at the second door on the right. "We're here."

Uncle Morten was holding up Lisbeth as she balanced stork-like on one leg, so Peter stepped up to the door and knocked three times. For a moment he thought maybe no one was home, so he knocked again. *Where do we go if they're not home?* he asked himself.

Then he heard a shuffling sound from inside the apartment. "Who is it?" came the faint voice of an older woman.

"It's me, *Mutti*," answered Lisbeth, using the German word for Mom. "And I brought some friends."

A latch clicked, and the door swung wide open. A small woman with gray hair pulled back in a bun stepped partway out. Wrinkles had overtaken her face, but she was trim and pretty in a green plaid dress. By the way her eyes were set—large and green—Peter could tell right away she was Lisbeth's mother.

"Lis!" she called happily. "I'm so glad that you could . . ." Her voice trailed off when she caught sight of her daughter, and her expression clouded over with worry.

"What's happened to you, Lis?" she croaked. "Have you been in an accident?" When she glanced at the others, her eyes widened even more. "And Morten, what are you—I thought you were . . ."

"We'll tell you everything, Mutti." Lisbeth reached over to take her mother's hand. "But can we come in?" She looked nervously down the hall, but no one else had seen them.

"Oh, of course, of course," replied her mother, pulling her inside. "Look at me, just standing here like a silly old woman. I'm sorry." She was clearly flustered at the sight of four hoboes standing at her door. "Come in, come in."

Everyone stepped inside the tidy little apartment. For a moment they all huddled in the small entry, while Mrs. von Schreider nervously wiped her hands on her white lace apron.

"Ernst!" she called back into the apartment. "Ernst! Lis is here, and she brought some friends."

"Oh, I . . . I'm sorry, mother," stuttered Lisbeth. "I should have introduced you. This is—"

Lisbeth's father came shuffling down the apartment's narrow hallway, and Lisbeth halted her introductions long enough to greet him.

"Lis!" he said, his voice catching on the edge of surprise. He was a slender, wiry man, not tall but well-built. Peter imagined he had probably been an athlete when he was younger, maybe a soccer player, and his face looked a lot like some of the portraits of von Schreiders hanging on the wall. Like his wife, he carried a good collection of wrinkles around his face. Smile wrinkles, Peter thought. Mr. von Schreider was smiling at the sight of his daughter, and he held his arms out.

"Oh, Dad!" Lisbeth gave her father a big hug. "I'm glad you're here."

Mr. von Schreider chuckled. "I'm glad you're here too, Lis, but you look . . . terrible!" He held her at arm's length by the shoulders. "Look at you! Two black eyes and your face is all puffy and scratched. Whatever happened?"

Lisbeth looked down and seemed embarrassed. "We'll tell you the whole story, Dad, but first I'd like you to meet some special friends of mine."

"Oh yes, of course, forgive me for ignoring our guests." Mr.

von Schreider straightened the well-worn striped robe he wore over his clothes, then he shook Peter's and Elise's hands warmly. "You're very welcome here. It looks as if you might want to clean up a bit."

"I . . . I apologize for showing up here in such a mess," Uncle Morten stammered as he took his turn shaking Mr. von Schreider's hand. "We didn't know where else to go."

"Please don't apologize," answered Lisbeth's father. "Lis's friends are always welcome here. But forgive me for asking . . . ah . . . I thought you might still be in prison?"

"Ernst!" scolded Lisbeth's mother. "Quit being so nosy. Morten doesn't need to tell us anything. Not just yet. Tell them about the planes."

"What? Oh yes, the planes," said Mr. von Schreider. "Yes, British. Can you believe it, Lis! They were so close we could almost wave to the pilots."

"He did wave," explained Lisbeth's mother. "I had to keep him from climbing out of the window."

"Brigitta!" Mr. von Schreider patted his wife's shoulder to make her stop.

"We saw them too, Dad." Lisbeth smiled, just barely. Then she was serious again. "We were sitting in Major Mueller's office—Peter, Elise, and I were there—just when they hit the old Shell Oil building. We were right there!"

It took a moment for Lisbeth's parents to understand what their daughter had just told them. Then her announcement sunk in, and Mrs. von Schreider clapped her hands to her mouth while she stared at her daughter. "You?" she asked. "Lis? You were in the building that was bombed? What were you doing there?"

"We're okay now." Uncle Morten stepped in to reassure them. "But you can be real proud of your daughter. She's been through a lot—including a sprained ankle!"

While the adults were talking Peter slipped over to the kitchen window to look down at the street. It was filled with bicyclists as before, but the German army truck was far down the street.

"Looks like they're gone now, Uncle Morten," he reported.

Morten nodded at his nephew. "Good, Peter," he answered back. "I thought so."

Then a movement down on the street caught Peter's eye, something in the shadows of a doorway. He stared at the shadow for several minutes, trying to make out a shape.

"Hey, Elise," Peter motioned with his hand. "Come here for a minute." The others were gathered around Lisbeth, who was sitting on a chunky little flowered sofa that seemed to take up half the floor in the apartment's front living room. Lisbeth was describing their escape, waving her hands for effect. Elise, still holding the cat, joined her brother at the window.

"You see that deep doorway with the steps down there next to the grocery?" Peter pointed.

"I think so," answered his sister. "What are you pointing at?"

"I think I saw someone down there, maybe the guy who was following us on the street on our way here."

"I never saw anyone following us, and I don't see anyone now."

Uncle Morten came up between them, leaned over the sink, and looked out the window. "What are you two looking at?" he asked.

"I'm trying to tell Elise that there's a guy down there watching us," said Peter. "But she won't believe me." He pointed out the window once more.

"Where?" asked Uncle Morten. Elise had given up and was going back into the living room.

"Right down—" Peter looked back again and squinted. The doorway was empty. "Oh, now I don't . . . he *was* there, Uncle Morten. It looked like the guy I saw following us earlier." Peter felt his ears getting hot. *No one believes me,* he fumed.

Uncle Morten stroked his unkempt beard and looked at Peter like a doctor examining a patient with an unknown disease. "Hmm. Maybe you'd better check down there once in a while . . . see if the guy comes back."

"He was there, Uncle Morten," insisted Peter. His ears were still hot. "I saw him."

"I know you did." He smiled at Peter, then turned to see Mrs. von Schreider bustling into the kitchen with an armload of towels. "But right now I think Lisbeth's mom wants us to wash up before we get her home dirty."

"You'll feel much better when you do," announced Mrs. von Schreider, pulling two small gray bath towels from the top. "We have two sinks, you know. One in the washroom, and the other in the kitchen."

Peter sighed, glancing once more out the window. He took the first turn washing up in the large kitchen sink while Uncle Morten headed for the washroom. Tiger sat down for his own cat bath on the weathered kitchen linoleum.

"Oh, look, Ernst," crooned Mrs. von Schreider. "He looks just like old Rudy, doesn't he?"

Mr. von Schreider stepped into the kitchen and crouched down to the floor. Then he clapped his hand on his knee, and the cat came over to rub his back on Mr. von Schreider's ankle.

"He likes you, Mr. von Schreider," mumbled Peter from under his towel.

The old man scratched Tiger behind the ears, and the cat turned on the loudest purr Peter had heard yet. "Which one of you does this little fellow belong to?" asked Mr. von Schreider.

"He's kind of an orphan," explained Peter. "I found him in the office part of the Shell House. Elise and I named him Tiger."

"And he made it through the bombing too?" asked Mr. von Schreider.

"I'm told he was the one who found me," boomed Uncle Morten, returning to the kitchen.

"It's true," explained Elise, who had traded places with Peter at the sink. "Uncle Morten was buried under a ceiling and we didn't even know he was there. Tiger's a hero."

"Is that so?" asked Mr. von Schreider, straightening up with a little grunt. His knees made a crackling sound as he did. "Well, all heroes deserve a reward." He called out to the living room, where Lisbeth and her mother were still talking in hushed tones. "Brigitta, don't you have a little cream in the ice box?"

"Yes, but I was saving it for—"

"For the hero," finished Mr. von Schreider, opening up the little white refrigerator that perched on four legs in the corner of the kitchen. "Ah ha," he said as he fished out a small pitcher. "For the hero."

Tiger was glad to please Mr. von Schreider and eagerly lapped up every drop the man poured into a saucer on the floor. "A little more, Tiger?" asked Lisbeth's father.

"Honestly, Ernst," observed Mrs. von Schreider, her arms crossed. "You and cats."

Mr. von Schreider shrugged. "They like me."

"Good thing," said Uncle Morten, looking cautiously toward Peter. Peter saw the look, and he guessed what his uncle was getting at.

"If you want your cat to stay here for a while," volunteered Mr. von Schreider with a kind smile, "we would be happy to take care of the animal for you until you can come back for him. As long as you like. Right, Brigitta?"

Mrs. von Schreider gave her husband a quick glance and then smiled a grandmotherly smile at Peter.

"Of course, Peter," she nodded. "It's up to you. But you can see that Lisbeth's father will be sure to take good care of the kitty."

Peter stroked the animal once more, took a deep breath, and nodded. The cat would be safe here with Lisbeth's parents. With another quick glance out the window, he wished he could feel as safe.

"Speaking of taking good care of things, Peter, you'd better have Lisbeth's mom look at that arm." Elise had been watching him. "That blood is really sick looking."

A minute later Peter was the patient, while Mrs. von Schreider made him take his shirt off and dabbed iodine on the long, jagged cut with a cotton ball. The sting took his breath away and made his eyes water, but he tried not to make a sound. In the corner of the room he could hear Uncle Morten talking to someone on the phone.

"Your chest too, Peter," Elise gasped. "Look at all those scratches from the cat!"

"Scratches?" Peter looked down at his chest for the first time. His sister was right. In all the running around, Tiger had left his mark.

"Well, you're the brave one, aren't you?" said Mrs. von Schreider as she dabbed at his chest. "I suppose you'll survive the cat attack. But you really could use some stitches in that arm. Let's just put this bandage on for now and see how it does. You'll forget all about it when you get some good food in your stomach."

Elise looked at the operation, made a face, and turned away. "Yech," she told him.

"Well, sorry!" He tried to swat at her with his towel, but only swiped her on the side. She hopped away, not noticing the papers from her pocket that fell to the floor. Peter leaned over to pick them up.

"Hey, look here," he said quietly as he unfolded the papers. They were drawings. The first was a fine, detailed close-up of a bed, with a vase of flowers on a table next to it. The others were even more lifelike, with faces and buildings, rooms and plates of food. "These are really good. Some of these look like the inside of a cell, like at the Shell House."

Elise glanced back over her shoulder, then whirled around to rescue her drawings. "You give those back, Peter Andersen!"

"I didn't do anything!" Peter held up his arms. "They just fell out of your pocket. But now I know who the mystery artist at the newspaper is."

Elise pointed straight at her brother and raised her eyebrows at him. "Not a word," she threatened.

Peter looked around to see if anyone had heard them. Mrs. von Schreider was busy putting away her iodine and supplies and seemed not to notice.

"I'll get you one of Ernst's old shirts," Lisbeth's mother told Peter as she slipped out of the room.

"Promise?" Elise held on to her stern look.

Peter shrugged. "I won't tell."

When Elise returned to the living room, Peter checked out the kitchen window once more. Every few minutes, army cars or ambulances raced by—but he didn't see anyone watching from the shadows across the street.

NOWHERE TO RUN

Uncle Morten leaned into the kitchen with the telephone at his ear and motioned for Peter to join him. "Hey, Peter, come here for a minute. Someone you need to talk to, but keep it quick."

Peter knew who it had to be, and he raced Elise to the phone. Elise got a head start, though, and grabbed it first. Peter leaned close and she held out the earpiece so Peter could hear.

"Mom? Dad?" she said.

"Is that you, Elise?" asked their father. The voice sounded far away. "Are you okay, honey?"

The next words poured out like a flood. "We're okay," she managed to explain. "It was all my fault—the Germans caught us because of the stupid fish, and we saw you and Grandfather coming to the building, but they lied to you—"

"Wait a minute, wait a minute," came their father's voice. "You can't tell me the whole story right now over the phone. But you and your brother are going to have a lot of explaining to do when you get home. *A lot* of explaining." Peter could tell when their father was upset by the way he repeated himself.

"I . . . I know, Dad, we're so sorry," said Elise. "We didn't mean for it to turn out like this."

"I'm sure you didn't. Now how about Peter? Where's your brother? Is he okay?"

"He's right here, Dad. He can hear you."

Peter called out so that his father could hear. "I'm okay, Dad. Just scraped up a little."

"Good. Now listen, both of you. I'm going to be there in Copenhagen just as fast as I can, do you understand? I believe there's a train leaving first thing in the morning, so I'll see you both early tomorrow. Just stay where you are." There was a pause. "Are you really okay? Your mother has been out of her mind these past few days." Another pause. "So have I."

Peter just wanted his father to be there right away so he could hang on to him the way he used to when he was a little boy. It didn't matter now that he was probably in more trouble than he had ever been in before. He just wanted to get home. Peter looked over at his sister, and she was crying.

"I'm sorry, Dad," Elise finally answered, choking back the tears. "Here's Peter."

She handed the phone to her brother, but Peter wasn't sure he could talk any better than Elise at that moment.

"Dad?" Peter sniffled.

"I'm here, son. Did you hear everything?"

"Yes, sir. I did."

"All right then. You heard me tell your sister that I'll be there as soon as I can. Just stay right where you are. Get some sleep."

"We won't go anywhere."

"I know, son. Why don't you put your uncle on the line again, and I'll see you in just a few hours, okay?"

"Right, Dad. I love you."

"I love you too."

Uncle Morten took the phone back and held on to Peter's shoulder with his big hand.

"Arne?" he spoke into the phone as if he had to yell all the way to Helsingor. "Arne? Look, one more thing before we hang up." He nodded. "Right. I told you what the kids went through. Uh-huh. You should have seen your daughter. Right. Both of them in fact. Well, I don't want to tell you what to do, but if you ask me I think they both deserve a lot of credit. Okay, I know you'll do the right thing. No, I'm not coming home right away. Yeah, we'll send word if we can. Lisbeth and I have to leave tonight for Sweden, so we won't see you in the morning. We have a contact with a boat. The kids should be fine here. Okay? Thanks, big brother."

Uncle Morten turned his head, said a couple more words into the phone, and hung up.

"What did Dad say?" asked Peter after his uncle had hung up the phone. "Was he still pretty upset?"

"Upset, yes," answered Uncle Morten, leaning against the kitchen counter. "But considering what his children have been doing, it's understandable. He should be here on the—whoa, cat!"

But it was too late. Tiger had already launched up from a chair to the kitchen counter at the smell of Mrs. von Schreider's dinner, and he was fishing his paw into a bowl of gravy.

From the other side of the room, Mrs. von Schreider threw a washrag at the animal. "That cat!" she yelled.

Mr. von Schreider came to the rescue, scooping up Tiger by the loose skin on his neck and carrying him like a baby to the sink. The cat had gravy all over his paws.

"He's just hungry. I told you, Brigitta. Here, Tiger, I'll get you something more to eat so you don't have to steal our gravy."

At the table, Lisbeth began to laugh, and the others joined in. Peter tried to forget what he had seen out on the street earlier, and he grinned. Still, he couldn't help peeking out the window once more while Mrs. von Schreider finished setting the table for dinner.

"Come on, Peter," Lisbeth urged him. "Sit down with us and help Elise tell your side of the story."

"Right now?"

"After we thank the Lord, of course," said Mr. von Schreider. "Daughter, would you?"

Lisbeth nodded. She was sitting with her leg propped up on a chair.

"Father, thank you for bringing us through ..." she blurted out with her head bowed. "Through everything. Thank you for Mutti and Dad, for letting Peter and Elise and Morten be here. For this food. You're so good to us. Thank you in Jesus' name. Amen."

Peter looked up to see Uncle Morten peeking at Lisbeth, grinning a silly grin. When he saw Peter, he gave him a wink.

After that, it didn't take long for Peter to realize how hungry he was. He tried not to take too much fish. And he took a deep, wonderful breath as the steaming plate of potatoes and gravy passed under his nose.

As she took a plate of food, Lisbeth reached over and put her hand on Peter's arm. "This week might not have turned out the way you expected, but Carlo was right, wasn't he?"

"Carlo?" Peter looked puzzled, trying to remember the name.

Lisbeth smiled. "I'm sorry. I introduced you to a lot of people at the Bible study. Carlo was the leader that night. He said God was in control of everything that happened to bring us together. Remember now?"

"I remember!" put in Elise, setting down her glass. "He said you were all praying for Uncle Morten, and that God was still in control. I wasn't too sure about that, though, when we saw you working in the Nazi headquarters in Helsingor. That was—"

"That was awful!" finished Peter. "First we thought for sure you were our friend, then we thought you were a traitor. It was pretty confusing for a while."

Lisbeth laughed once more, and everyone laughed with her. With Lisbeth's help, Peter and Elise explained the whole story over dinner. Peter guessed from all the gasps and shocked expressions that Lisbeth's parents had never heard anything about her working with the Resistance before. Even Uncle Morten's eyes grew wide when Lisbeth told how she called her friends in the Resistance with secret information, and about how she called Peter and Elise's father when the twins had been captured.

"The Nazis thought I was a wonderful secretary," explained Lisbeth. "Probably because of my German name and the way I could speak German. It took a long time for them to figure out that I was really working for the Resistance."

"And I thought it was just a nice office job you had there in Helsingor," said Lisbeth's mother as she passed around a plate of cabbage. She hovered over her guests, making sure they had enough. Peter guessed she had emptied her cupboards to feed them. There was even a small serving of cod for everyone.

Lisbeth smiled at her mother. "I never told them I had two anti-Nazi parents, Mutti. I didn't want to get you mixed up in anything, in case they ever wanted to check on my family."

"Well, I thank you for that!" declared Lisbeth's mother, dishing another small potato onto Uncle Morten's plate. "Because if they knew how much your father hated what the Nazis are doing to our country—"

Lisbeth's father "harumphed" from his chair. He puffed his cheeks out as he spoke. "When we came here after the first war, you were just a small girl, Lis. I love this place, and it just makes me sick to see what has happened because of that madman Hitler!"

"I know, Dad." Lisbeth took her father's hand and patted it. "I know. Just be careful what you say around those people."

"Careful, she says." He turned to his wife. "This girl comes limping home with two black eyes, half dead, those stupid Nazis out looking for her, and bombs going off over her head. And she tells *me* to be careful."

Mr. von Schreider shook his head, sighed, and gave his daughter a worried look. Then he leaned under the table for something. "I'm just glad you're here, Lis."

"Ernst!" cried Mrs. von Schreider. "I've seen that kind of move before. Are you feeding your fish to the cat?"

Mr. von Schreider just smiled at his wife and shrugged. "We have to help the poor fellow feel at home, don't we? He's been through a lot, from what the children tell us."

Lisbeth's mother still wasn't satisfied. "If the cat stays here, he's going to take his meals somewhere else."

Peter had to smile too. *I think Tiger's going to have a good home,* he thought. After a bit he cleared his plate and stood up with Elise to stack dishes by the sink. Once more, Peter stood on his tiptoes by the sink and looked out the window down at the sidewalk. It was almost dark, but what he saw made his stomach turn a somersault.

"Uncle Morten," Peter said nervously. Uncle Morten was again telling the story of how they had escaped the burning building.

"Hang on, Peter, I'm just telling Lisbeth's dad—"

"Uncle Morten, I think you'd better see this." The way Peter spoke and waved his hand made Uncle Morten frown and get up from his chair.

"What is it?"

"Those soldiers down there," Peter explained. "They're back, and there's a bunch of them."

Peter's uncle, Elise, and Mr. von Schreider crowded up to the window to see where Peter was pointing.

"There, you see them?" Peter kept his eye on one group. "They're going into people's apartments now." *And we don't have anywhere else left to run,* he thought.

"They're looking for something, all right," Uncle Morten finally muttered. "Did you see them come up to this building yet, Peter?"

"Not yet, but I'm not sure." Peter looked pale again. "I think they're still on the other side of the street, a few doors down." He pointed to a group of four soldiers in gray helmets coming quickly out of a store, then sank back down into a kitchen chair with a nervous sigh. He decided he had been wrong about feeling safe and comfortable. Lisbeth's laughing had almost made him forget there was someone down on the street looking for them.

"Okay, we've been through this cat-and-mouse stuff before," Uncle Morten reminded his nephew. "God's in control, remember?"

Peter knew his uncle was right. Still, it was hard to keep his hands from shaking. He nodded. "I know He is."

Uncle Morten raised his eyebrows, as if he hadn't expected Peter to agree.

There are a lot of things you don't know about me, Uncle Morten, thought Peter. He wished he could explain about the way he believed now, how last summer he had prayed to follow Jesus, but Uncle Morten turned quickly to Lisbeth's father.

"I'm sorry, sir, for putting you and Mrs. von Schreider through this. It's not fair to you. We need to leave."

"Nonsense," interrupted Lisbeth's father. "And go where? If any idiot soldiers come to the door, we'll just have a nice chat."

Mr. von Schreider smiled bravely, then turned away. Peter was the only one who noticed that he closed his eyes and sighed. Uncle Morten kept watch out the window, and Peter jumped when the phone rang.

"What do you mean, my guests had better leave?" Mr. von Schreider asked the caller. Peter could hear another man's voice buzzing from the phone receiver. "Soldiers, in our building already? Yes, of course I know what you're talking about. How did you? Well, I appreciate the warning. Thank you."

Before Mr. von Schreider had hung up Uncle Morten was already in action.

"Thank your neighbor for us," Uncle Morten whispered to Lisbeth's father. Then he grabbed Peter's arm as they went out to the living room.

"Girls!" he whispered, with an urgent wave of his hand. "They're in the building now." He didn't have to explain who "they" were. A minute later, "they" were pounding on the door.

"Open up here," commanded a gruff, muffled German voice.

"Open up!" Peter could hear the same command up and down the hallway, and more banging.

Everyone froze for a moment until Uncle Morten motioned for Peter and Elise to follow him down the hall.

"The closet," whispered Lisbeth, and the four of them piled into a hall closet the size of a small phone booth. Peter sat down on a neat pile of shoes in the back next to Elise. A long wool coat that smelled of extra-strength mothballs hung in his face. Uncle Morten and Lisbeth stood wedged together just inside the door. In the front room, Peter could hear Mr. von Schreider shuffling to the front door while the German pounded and pounded.

"I'm coming, I'm coming," rasped the old man, not in Danish but in his native German. Peter held his breath, straining to hear what was going on, and he heard Mr. von Schreider unbolt the door and swing it open.

"Welcome, come in!" said Lisbeth's father, sounding like a jolly German Santa. "What brings you boys here this afternoon? What can we do for you?"

"Oh, excuse me," came the soldier's voice. "I'm sorry to bother you." He sounded much more polite than Peter had heard German soldiers talk to Danish people before.

"No bother at all," came Mr. von Schreider. "Are you in a hurry, or can you come in for a cup of tea? It's nice to have someone to speak German with for a change."

"No, I'm afraid we don't have time for tea tonight," answered a voice Peter thought he recognized. The hair on the back of Peter's neck stood on end. "But thank you. We're just checking the neighborhood. I have some information that a man, a woman, and two teenagers—saboteurs—are hiding in the general area."

"Oh, really?" asked Mr. von Schreider. "Did one of our people see them?"

"They were followed to this neighborhood from the Shell House, I believe," answered the man. Now Peter was sure he recognized the voice. Then he remembered something that made him bite his finger.

"My shirt," Peter whispered into the coat next to him, where Elise was hiding. He thought for a chilling second about his old shirt he had left on the kitchen floor. Did he remember to pick it up? "My shirt's out there."

"Shh," whispered Elise, poking Peter in the ribs. "I threw it in the trash."

Peter let out his breath, but not too loudly. It sounded as if Lisbeth's father was still trying to make small talk with the soldiers.

"Terrible what's happened there with the British and their bombs, eh?" Mr. von Schreider sounded disgusted. "We need to hit them back, hard."

One of the other young soldiers laughed. "That's right, old man. Hey, Mr. Poulsen, I like the way this fellow thinks."

Peter heard Elise catch her breath when she heard the name.

"Yes, yes," came the familiar voice. He sounded nervous. "I wish it were so easy. Just reach out this kitchen window here and pluck them out of the sky."

Everyone laughed—but it was a stiff, formal laugh. Peter could tell no one thought it was very funny. Then Mr. Poulsen spoke up again, and this time he sounded as if he were out in the kitchen. Peter put his head under Uncle Morten's legs so he could get his ear closer to the closet door and hear better.

"Nice drawings here," said Mr. Poulsen. Peter closed his eyes tightly and gritted his teeth. He was afraid to tell Elise he must have left her pictures out on the kitchen table. Everything had happened too quickly. "Very talented artist. You did them? Looks like someplace I've seen before."

"Oh, that?" Mr. von Schreider obviously didn't know what to say, since he had never seen the drawings before. "They're, well, they're nothing. A friend did them. Just for amusement. Just a hobby. They're nothing really."

"Oh, I disagree," said Mr. Poulsen. "They're quite well done. Be sure to tell her—I mean, your friend—that they're very good."

The voices came closer once more, and then Mr. Poulsen

spoke to a soldier. "You can tell your captain there's nothing in here, Sergeant. Just German friends. Why don't you try the next floor? I have to use the washroom here, and then I'm going to report back to Colonel Ludheim. We'll find those saboteurs."

"And you boys come back when you have more time to visit, won't you?" called Mr. von Schreider. "We'll fix you something hot next time."

"*Danke.* Thanks," replied a soldier, his voice echoing beyond the front door. Then the front door slammed shut, and Mr. Poulsen lowered his voice.

"Say, pardon me for asking, but is the washroom right down the hall there?"

Peter could barely make out Mrs. von Schreider's trembling voice. "Yes, it's at the end of the hall."

Mr. Poulsen's steps came closer to the closet, and he paused for a moment in front of the closet door. The shoes Peter was sitting on had become very hard and uncomfortable, but he didn't dare move—or even breathe.

"Very nice sketches of the Shell House," Mr. Poulsen told no one in particular. His voice was almost a whisper, and Peter was sure the von Schreiders couldn't hear him. "Very nice indeed. She'll be a fine artist." The man continued on toward the bathroom, and was back out in a moment. Peter tried to think of what to do, but his mind wouldn't work. *How did Mr. Poulsen know to come here?* Peter asked himself over and over. *Somebody* did *follow us. He knows we're here!*

Mr. Poulsen stopped again in front of the closet. A moment later the door flew open and they were blinking in horror at Mr. Poulsen standing in the hallway, pointing an evil-looking black German pistol straight at Peter's face. No one moved.

"Now, very slowly," ordered Mr. Poulsen in a steady voice. "Please just step out of the closet and come sit down on the sofa for a moment."

GOODBYE IN THE RAIN

"Well," said Mr. Poulsen after everyone had filed out of the closet. Uncle Morten helped Lisbeth to the sofa, while Elise and Peter sat on the floor. "This is quite a group."

He kept the gun leveled at them as he moved to the front door. With one eye always on Uncle Morten, he cracked open the door and checked the outside hallway. Satisfied that no one was there, he turned back to Mr. and Mrs. von Schreider, who were standing nervously out in the kitchen.

"Please don't blame yourselves," he told them with a smile that Peter had seen before. It looked sickeningly sweet and out of place. "You both did a fine job of hiding your friends."

"What do you want, Poulsen?" demanded Uncle Morten. Peter was sitting with his back to his uncle's legs, and he could imagine Uncle Morten springing up to tackle the man.

"Relax, Morten," said Mr. Poulsen. "Relax. This isn't what you think it is. But you're really still in prison if you stop to think a moment. You can't get out of this building—out of this city even—without my help. And I'm going to get you out of here, whether you like it or not."

Uncle Morten squinted his eyes at the man, who still held them prisoner with a gun. "So where are you taking us?"

Mr. Poulsen smiled again. "Of course you don't trust me. No reason to, after all the times we've chatted in the prison. But this is different. The children are going home now, and you two adults . . . well, you're going to wherever it is you need to go. And we're all going to ride out of here in my car, like one happy family."

"If you're taking us back to the Nazis, why don't you just call for the soldiers right now?" asked Uncle Morten.

Mr. Poulsen nervously cracked open the front door once more, then turned to them with a fire in his eyes. He waved the gun at them as he talked.

"You still don't get it, do you, fisherman? I'm trying to help you people, and all you do is complain."

Peter had heard Mr. Poulsen say something like that before, back at the Shell House—when the man was trying to get them to tell about their friends at the Underground newspaper. He was either a good actor, or very mixed up about whose side he was on.

"Why are you doing this?" Peter found himself asking. When Mr. Poulsen looked at him, he regretted letting it slip.

"Why? You're just like my boy back home in Helsingor," answered Mr. Poulsen. He smiled for an instant, but still gripped the gun with white knuckles as he walked closer. Peter noticed he was sweating, and the hand holding the gun was shaking. "Always asking why. I thought of Keld being held in a prison made for criminals, like the one you were in. But of course his mother won't ever let me see him now. Not a visit, not even a phone call. I think she destroys my letters."

What's he talking about? thought Peter. Mr. Poulsen was a strange, sad person—hard to understand.

"Why am I helping you?" Mr. Poulsen shook his head. "We were only supposed to keep you for a few hours, but things got out of hand with the colonel. Maybe this whole war has gotten out of hand."

Then he looked out the door again and seemed to snap out of his dream. "And I'm still Danish. Look, here's what I'm going to do for you. You can trust me or not, I don't care. We're going to go in my car back to Helsingor. You're not going to make it out of this building without my help. The kids, the Germans could care less about, but they *are* looking for the fisherman."

Peter and Elise looked at their uncle, wondering what he would do. Would he trust Mr. Poulsen?

"So take me and leave them here," said Uncle Morten.

"Oh, but it's not that simple, my friend," replied the nervous Mr. Poulsen. "I said we are all going together, and that's what I meant. Home to Helsingor. Isn't that what you want?"

"Then you're not giving us a choice?" asked Lisbeth.

"You understand me well."

Lisbeth turned back to her parents, who had been standing in the kitchen like statues.

"Mutti?"

Mrs. von Schreider carefully stepped over and gave her daughter a hug. Mr. von Schreider was right behind her.

"We'll keep praying for you," Lisbeth's father assured her. The others said nothing, in a sort of nervous silence. He looked up with a stern expression at Mr. Poulsen and his gun. "And you, I don't know what you are. You're certainly not a real Dane. But we'll pray for you too."

Mr. Poulsen only blinked at Lisbeth's father, then turned to the others. "Enough talk. Fisherman, you help your girlfriend. And the two kids, you stay right behind them. We're going down the stairs and out the back door."

Peter thought there were still soldiers in the building, but he didn't dare protest. Mrs. von Schreider disappeared for a moment and returned with an armload of three sweaters and a coat.

"Here, these are extra ones I've been saving," she told Elise.

"Maybe they won't fit you, but they're better than nothing. You put one of them on."

Elise smiled at Lisbeth's mother and took one of the sweaters. "Thank you, Mrs. von Schreider. Thank you for everything."

Mr. Poulsen was fidgeting with his pistol and shifting from one foot to the other. "Let's go!" he demanded.

"We're ready," replied Uncle Morten, looking back at Peter and Elise. "Stay close, kids."

Then he pulled Lisbeth's arm around his shoulder to keep the weight off her ankle and stepped through the door as Mr. Poulsen opened it. A minute later they were limping slowly and quietly down the bare, dark hallway toward the stairs.

They went down the stairs the same way they had come up—slowly and one at a time. At the bottom landing, Mr. Poulsen checked for soldiers out the front door, though by then it was quite dark. He held his gun pointed through his long, black overcoat so everyone could still see it.

"They must be in other buildings by now," he whispered. "Around the corner to the left. My car is on the side street."

There was really no need to whisper—no one was out on the dark, drizzly street. Peter shivered as they stepped out into the chilled night air.

"This one." Mr. Poulsen finally pointed at a newer black sedan. They could have guessed. It looked like a German car, and it was practically the only one on the block.

"Now, Morten, I'd like you to drive us, while I sit up in the front passenger seat to give you directions."

"I know the way," growled Uncle Morten.

"Yes, well, just the same, I'd like to see where we're going. The others can sit in the back."

No one answered, but everyone did as they were told. Mr. Poulsen was following every move Uncle Morten made with his gun.

Peter had never been inside a car like this before. It was one of those larger models with the big backseats that were taller than his father's giant easy chair at home and three times as wide. Uncle Morten got in on the driver's side after helping Lisbeth in the back door, while Peter followed his sister into the backseat on the other side. Peter was just about to shut the door when he felt something furry rubbing against his legs. He couldn't see it in the dark, but he knew in an instant what it was. Somehow Tiger had slipped out the door of the apartment to follow them!

Elise must have noticed too, because she jumped and almost made a noise. But Peter tightened his grip on her elbow and in one movement scooped up the cat in his free hand. A second later they were all sitting in the backseat, and Peter did his best to keep Tiger down on the floor between his ankles.

"I trust you still remember how to drive?" Mr. Poulsen asked Uncle Morten. He glanced back quickly at the three in the backseat, but kept the gun trained on Uncle Morten.

Uncle Morten couldn't find where to put the key right away. He jammed it several ways before he found the right place.

"It's been five years since I've been behind the wheel, thanks to your German buddies," he muttered.

"You'll remember just fine, I'm sure," answered Mr. Poulsen.

Tiger started playing with Peter's shoelace, and Peter wiggled his foot to keep the cat busy.

"Sit still back there, would you?" ordered Mr. Poulsen, sounding irritated.

"Uh, sure," replied Peter as Uncle Morten finally got the car started and jerked to a start. Elise's head whipped back into the seat while everyone grabbed for something to hang on to.

"Sorry," said Uncle Morten. "I'm a little rusty at this."

Mr. Poulsen kept the pistol pointed at Peter's uncle as he leaned back against the passenger door. "Just get us there. If anyone stops us, let me do the talking."

"Forty-five minutes to Helsingor," said Uncle Morten as he steered slowly out of the city and north along the shore road toward their home. "Where do we stop?"

"I thought you understood this by now," answered the dark

figure of Mr. Poulsen. "I've been instructed to follow and bring back anyone who escaped the Shell House. But with your help, now I can do better than that. Now we're going to track down the miserable fishboat captains who are taking all you people across to Sweden in their boats. Finally they're going to get what they deserve. And you're going to introduce me to your friends with the boat."

"Boat?" asked Uncle Morten.

Now Peter understood exactly what Mr. Poulsen wanted. He didn't want to help them. He just wanted to use Uncle Morten and Lisbeth as bait to trap more Underground people.

"If you think I'm just going to drive you to wherever you want, then—"

"My dear fisherman," interrupted Mr. Poulsen. Now his voice had the cold edge Peter had heard back at the Shell House. "Perhaps you're forgetting who is holding the gun, and who is sitting in the backseat of this car. I am prepared to use this thing. It would not be pleasant."

There has to be something we can do, thought Peter, *besides just sit here and let him get away with this.*

Peter looked over at Lisbeth. Even in the dark he could make out her stiff expression. Once in a while she would rub her forehead, and Mr. Poulsen kept glancing back at her.

Beside him, Elise looked over at Peter and raised her eyebrows as if to say that she didn't know what to do either. And as they got closer and closer to home Peter could only grip the door handle tighter and tighter in frustration. Tiger was very tired of staying hidden next to their feet.

"Say, what is going on down there on the floor anyway?" Mr. Poulsen finally asked. "Do you two have foot problems or something?"

Tiger had finally had enough. As Mr. Poulsen glanced over the seat the cat rocketed straight into his face, claws first.

Peter wasn't sure who was more surprised—Tiger or Mr.

Poulsen. Tiger yowled and spit; Mr. Poulsen hit the ceiling. Elise screamed. Even Peter jumped.

In the next moment of confusion, the cat must have jumped on Uncle Morten, because the car went skidding sideways on the slick road. With fur flying everywhere, Peter tried to grab for the cat in front. All he came up with was someone's head—Mr. Poulsen's head—and he held on tight around the man's face.

A second later the car slammed sideways into something with a sickening crunch. The car shook, then tipped up on two wheels. The glass in Peter's door shattered and fell all over his lap. Peter thought they were going to flip over for a moment, but he held on tight and they came back down with a heavy bounce. He was afraid of what he had grabbed in the front seat, but was more afraid to let go.

"The gun!" yelled Uncle Morten, and he grabbed at Mr. Poulsen's hand like a snake snapping up its dinner.

"Elise," yelled Peter. "Help me hold him!"

Elise and Lisbeth leaned over the back of the seat to join Peter while Uncle Morten twisted Mr. Poulsen's wrist and pulled the gun from his grip. Tiger was dancing from person to person, adding more confusion to the panic. But there was no shot.

"I've got it," announced Uncle Morten after a few seconds. Peter still had his hands clamped tightly around Mr. Poulsen's eyes while Elise had grabbed the collar of the man's coat. He was kind of roaring, trying to wave his arms.

"All right," said Uncle Morten, in control once more. "Is everyone okay? You can let him go now."

This time it was Uncle Morten who held the gun, and Peter gladly let go of Mr. Poulsen. Tiger had returned to the backseat and was licking his paws as if nothing had happened. Peter shook off the glass from the window.

"What kind of . . ." sputtered Mr. Poulsen. "Something in my face . . ."

"Never mind that." Uncle Morten snapped on the overhead

light. "The situation has changed now. Lisbeth, can we find something to tie this man up with?"

"I think so," answered Lisbeth from the backseat.

"Maybe we can tear off one of the sleeves of this sweater," volunteered Elise.

"No need to trouble yourself," said Mr. Poulsen, his old voice returning. "You'll find the gun is not loaded."

"Sure," answered Uncle Morten. "You're not going to bluff your way out of this one, Poulsen. I want you to slide out of the door very slowly."

"I'm not joking," insisted Mr. Poulsen. "See for yourself."

Before Uncle Morten could check the pistol, Mr. Poulsen yanked at the door handle, put all his weight on the crushed door, and forced it open with a screech of twisted metal. He stumbled outside into the darkness.

"Hold it!" shouted Uncle Morten as he slid out after the man. In the half light from inside the car, Peter saw his uncle point the gun up into the sky. All they heard was a clicking sound. By then Mr. Poulsen was scrambling off into a field next to what looked like a cluster of small homes. A light came on inside one of the buildings.

"He wasn't kidding about the gun, was he?" asked Peter from inside the car.

Uncle Morten took a few steps into the darkness in the direction Mr. Poulsen had disappeared, then looked back at them. He again pointed the gun at the sky and pulled the trigger several more times. Nothing. He tossed the useless gun back onto the front seat.

"No, for once he was telling the truth. What an odd duck."

Peter and Elise tumbled over the front seat to see outside, but Uncle Morten pushed them back.

"Let's get out of here," urged Uncle Morten, "before Poulsen gets to a phone or finds one of his friends."

Uncle Morten started the engine, yanked the gearshift through some horrible grinding sounds, jerked the car back and forth, and sped off down the road.

"Sorry, kids," Uncle Morten told them as they picked up speed. The car groaned and squeaked, and there was a piece of metal dragging somewhere underneath. "Elise, hang on to Peter so he doesn't fall out the door."

"I've got him," answered Elise. Her hands were tight around Peter's shoulders, almost pinning him against the front seat.

"Thanks, Elise," said Peter. "Just don't choke me."

Peter could hear the splashing of the car against wet pavement through the crack in the front door he was holding shut. By the way it was all twisted up, he wasn't sure how Mr. Poulsen had even forced it open. There was surely no way it would close again. If they could just get a piece of rope, they could tie it shut.

This time they didn't have far to go. Peter couldn't see any landmarks clearly, but he could tell they were only a few minutes from home.

"Hey, Peter, Elise," Uncle Morten called out over the road noise and the complaining car. "Lisbeth and I have to keep going to catch a boat, so we have to just drop you off. Understand?"

"Don't forget the cat, Morten," Lisbeth leaned forward in her seat. "They have to take the cat."

Peter thought he heard a tiny chuckle from his uncle. "Oh yeah, right," said Uncle Morten. "The cat. Don't forget that cat!"

Tiger was still nervous about his ride in the car, jumping from lap to lap.

"Look, I see the Saint Olai Church steeple!" cried Elise, almost letting go of her brother. They were almost home.

They drove past familiar dark buildings, and soon Uncle Morten pulled over to the curb in front of Peter and Elise's apartment. He left the motor running.

"Blink the light twice when you get upstairs to show me you're okay, will you?" he asked.

Peter could only lean over and give his uncle a hug. He felt Lisbeth's hand on his shoulder.

"Take good care of your sister now," Lisbeth told him from the darkness of the backseat.

"And tell your dad we'll be home soon," added Uncle Morten.

"Okay, but when will—" began Peter.

"No time now," Peter's uncle interrupted. "Go. Take your cat."

"I have him," said Elise softly as she slipped out of the backseat and into the cold drizzle.

They both stepped through puddles on the sidewalk and in a minute were climbing up the stairway to their apartment on the second floor. Out of habit, Peter counted the stairs. Sixteen, seventeen, eighteen. It didn't seem real, and his mind raced. In another minute he and Elise would have to explain everything to their parents.

He patted the Bible in his back pocket as he climbed. He remembered Frank's voice from the prison cell.

"Just imagine the words on the page," Frank had told him. "Now close your eyes and read them."

Peter kept his hand on the Bible, closed his eyes, and once more recited the ancient promise in a quiet whisper. Somehow it seemed to make sense out of this crazy day.

"When you pass through the rivers, they will not sweep over you. When you walk through the fire, you will not be burned . . ."

"What did you say, Peter?" came Elise's voice from behind.

Twenty-five, twenty-six, twenty-seven. Peter smiled to himself, took a deep breath, hopped up the last three steps, and reached out to knock on their front door.